Hooks

Hook

Julie Oakes

DUNDURN
TORONTO

es, 2012

son Hirst
esse Hooper
Webcom

ary and Archives Canada Cataloguing in Publication

Oakes, Julie, 1948-
    Hooks / by Julie Oakes.

Also issued in electronic format.
ISBN 978-1-4597-0156-4

    I. Title.

PS8579.A54H65 2012   C813'.54   C2011-905999-1

1   2   3   4   5   16   15   14   13   12

Conseil des Arts   Canada Council
du Canada   for the Arts

Canadä

ONTARIO ARTS COUNCIL
CONSEIL DES ARTS DE L'ONTARIO

We acknowledge the support of the **Canada Council for the Arts** and the **Ontario Arts Council** for
our publishing program. We also acknowledge the financial support of the **Government of Canada**
through the **Canada Book Fund** and **Livres Canada Books**, and the **Government of Ontario** through
the **Ontario Book Publishing Tax Credit** and the **Ontario Media Development Corporation**.

Care has been taken to trace the ownership of copyright material used in this book. The author
and the publisher welcome any information enabling them to rectify any references or credits in
subsequent editions.

J. Kirk Howard, President

All illustrations by Julie Oakes.

Printed and bound in Canada.
www.dundurn.com

Dundurn
3 Church Street, Suite 500
Toronto, Ontario, Canada
M5E 1M2

Gazelle Book Services Limited
White Cross Mills
High Town, Lancaster, England
LA1 4XS

Dundurn
2250 Military Road
Tonawanda, NY
U.S.A. 14150

For my parents, Donovan and Joyce Cowan

Hooker — *n (1567) 1: one that hooks 2: prostitute*

Preface

Georgia

"Fifty rupees for a penetration!"

Bernie had literally barked it. He has an obtuse social sense, as if he doesn't understand what might be offensive or off-putting and just blurts out whatever pops into his head. He is the guy who has to say, in front of other people, that there is egg on your face as if he is doing you a service of honesty. In fact, he just doesn't have the inner patience to wait, ask for an aside, and then quietly whisper the eggy news. It is Bernie's way — slightly off-key — as if he's not really in sync with himself. It's the side of Americans that Europeans understandably veer away from but which Americans deem endearingly idiosyncratic. Bernie is, in his own way, generous, even earnest with his desire to communicate, but he is also egocentrically insensitive and it was getting on my nerves that he seemed to find it necessary to repeatedly and so loudly proclaim the sordid details of this new book proposal. I had suspected the authenticity of the project from the get-go and, although I had accepted the assignment because I was avid for experience, I knew that Bernie's motivations had more to do with sensationalism and a big dollar.

I had been hired to write a coffee-table book on prostitution in India, and Bernie, my publisher, had thrown a party in his uptown New York loft for my going-away. His wife Sharma — she's East Indian, from Hyderabad — is his link to what will be my host organization in India, Urban Help. They work with street people, including prostitutes. Everyone was there, my friends, his friends, and those who were probably neither of our friends hovering in the sycophant wings ready to find the flaw that they could use to pull down my dubious research. Those who had been to India agreed that, indeed, I should listen for this — "fifty rupees for a penetration!" — for it signalled the availability of prostitutes from the lower classes. Bernie's evident pleasure at the notice he had gained following his bombastic delivery was unsavoury, and when Bernie illuminated his guests with the exchange rate — that fifty rupees was worth about one dollar in our American money — I felt a further irritation, a nudge of shame at the advance I had been given.

In the beginning, when Bernie had first outlined his plan to have me do the text for a book on prostitution in India, I had doubts about accepting his proposal. Sharma convinced me, really. I explained to her that I have a higher goal for my writing and she said, "It furthers one to have somewhere to go." She said it was from the I Ching.

The geography of this writing game is brutal. I am known as an ethnographer noted for my willingness to research risky situations. I want to go deeper than reportage. I don't really care that people think that I am ambitious and self-centred as I take on these projects. I have been criticized as being little more than a "sensationalist." Such a critique would be a moot point, yet at moments I also doubt my depth. I believe transgressive behaviour can be useful for study and it is why I tempt fate. The low end of human behaviour has a hypnotizing attraction, but I am clear on one point — I have not performed what I consider to be acts of indignity; I have stopped my research at a boundary of my own choosing that keeps my ethical self intact.

I confess. I'm a "sublime" addict, ever wanting the next fix of "beyond." It is my weakness to be seduced by offers that I make to myself and, as a result, to go beyond the pale of most people's acceptance level. I actually look on it as a kind of stoicism. The journeys I embark upon are precarious, for although I may accept these challenges to engage, I am not positive as to the exact location of my moral line, that boundary which, when confronted, I must refuse to cross. Hence, I often walk on eggshells in these realms I elect to inhabit.

I look down on a form of avoidance, termed "moral," as a rather self-righteous complacency to accept certain taboos that society has set. One of these taboos is against information about and visualizations of sex. A long and complex history of precedents set by the needs of survival, religion, and socialization can, I'm sure, be argued on the subject of sexual taboos but, be they relevant and wise or just habitually supported in a lazy sense of resisting change, I, personally, am sufficiently curious to want to explore. Prostitution may be sordid to others, but to me it's Interesting, big "I" interesting.

I feel like I have had a perpetual awareness of transgression. One of my earliest, albeit vague, memories is of a group of men, burly, spitting tobacco, rude talking, and leering as they cheered on a Clydesdale mounting a mare. What is an even vaguer memory is an incident — I believe that same day, for the memory is coupled with the mating scene — in a basement, coal-dust dark, when the woolly smell of trousers damp from a foggy day overcame my fear of a possible transgression. I think I remember this, but I'm not positive.

My last assignment from Bernie Morgan of Morgan, Miller, and Sheinmann, was to come up with the text for a book on the sex clubs in New York City. I would doll up and head out to all sorts of venues — peep shows, S&M clubs, singles, lesbian, and gay clubs where there was live sex to be had in the back rooms, strip bars, and escort agencies — all as if I was a seasoned regular. I would often join in the action. It was necessary in order to be believable in my role-playing. I would wipe out any real involvement in these excursions by penning the experiences after they were had, which purged me and excused me emotionally for having to commit to them. I felt like two persons: one who participated and the other who reported on this participating person. Curiosity served as the source of my mettle during my research but it was all quite risky and it got to me, for it became a chore trying to stay positive in the midst of dysfunctional detachment. Also, I had experienced some close calls, physically, for I am small enough to be a vulnerable target for mischief, and although my ethical self is different from the norm, I did not want to experience harm.

I was lucky. I came out the other side with accolades, and now Bernie feels we can top our mutual success with this current scheme of his. I have had a long enough respite. I, too, want back in the game but I will not be partaking in the action this time, only observing in the hopes of understanding and then turning it into something, into art, into something more than just a coffee-table book. I turn to my fascination with the Enlightenment dynamic when De Sade took curiosity overboard in the name of man's right to know and experience everything. I figure it is this woman's turn to know.

"Who would want to buy such a book?" The decent moral majority might well ask but the answer was very clear to Bernie and his partners when they reviewed the sales of my first book. Evidently, there is a very large portion of the public who want to know about things they aren't willing to observe or experience firsthand.

My peculiar heat is a desire to tempt a risky prospect. I can picture the world with an entirety that includes malevolence and I have known, from an early age, that the devil can skirt close so it is best to know a little of his character in advance to prepare for the times when the dealings with darkness come closer. Bernie is not the only one who is "using." I am also using him and his validation to slake my own thirst.

When I did the first book with Bernie, was I doing ethno-graphic research into sexuality or simply justifying abnormal behaviour with the term "research"? I choose the term, now as I did then, to account for any doubts that might arise at my methods to gain information in my quest for a conscious-ness that contains perversity. I am standing up for my right to research an area that has the hex of a taboo and I am as ada-mant as ever about my ability to carry through this task with my psyche intact.

I am writing this forward before I begin, to see later if my anticipation matches the results. What am I expecting to find? I believe that if I keep my eyes and ears open and exercise a certain awareness of the immediate, then I will comprehend the meaning of the moment. The fact that I will be in a country of more than one and a half billion people, looking for connections, might seem an impossibility but this is exactly where I *should* find insights. If I watch with mindfulness, the connections will resonate, especially as I have the added advantage of the objective illumination of culture shock.

"Fifty rupees for a penetration!" Bernie had to repeat it, again and again, so I made rapid apologies, gave Sharma a big hug, and was propelled out into the New York streets with a round of well-wishing, but as at any fête where the social spot-light is intense, I had run out of smiles. I could perform no longer.

Now, here I am, high in the sky above a black ocean with "Fifty rupees for a penetration" looping through my head. I feel slightly nervous and almost sick from sitting so long but I'm also excited, eager to "research prostitution in India." Quite the concept.

I remember the story that Bernie told me of a man who, as a tourist in India, had been drinking in a Mumbai bar. He had felt a passing hand press his sweating cheek.

"You are always sweating in India. You will see. It's good for your skin," Bernie had said. "But also, the pores, they become wider. From a palmed piece of soaked paper, this pat on the cheek had transmitted a drug that was absorbed through his skin. Dermal toxicity! He passed out and next morning awoke to find himself in a hospital. They said that he had been found outside a bar by "helpful" men who brought him in to the hospital. Ha! He had been bandaged. They said he had been stabbed. He later discovered that he no longer had a pancreas. It seemed there had been a period of illness once he returned to New York and they discovered this was the reason. Not only was he missing a vital organ that was being hawked on a black market, but the aspect of AIDS loomed large, for he had been cut open, and unfortunately he did test HIV Positive. Dirty buggers. India is a serious country."

"You must pledge to me that you will hone your street smarts — you're a little too trusting — and be alert to messages received through your proximity sense. In some ways, I'm hesitant to send a woman out there but you've a gift for getting close to people, Georgia. I'll be sending out a photographer at some point, once you've gotten into the scene. I'm not sure who it will be yet. Just be careful. Don't tempt fate."

It's February 3, 2003. On the world front, the American president, George W. Bush, is threatening Iraq. The British prime minister, Tony Blair, has pledged his indivisible support. The Muslim fundamental terrorist group Al Qaeda has been linked to Saddam Hussein, and rumours are flying. It seems like the world is in a lurid heat, a suspended bloodlust, looking to rough up the enemy, whoever they may be.

I am heading to India to research prostitution, in a world that seems ready for war. My thoughts turn to Lot's wife, who could not resist her fatal turn. I do not want to become a pillar of salt. Sordid imaginings. I pull up the blind and look beyond the wing at utter darkness.

Karma

Memsahib is an American, from New York City. She embodies many of the ideas that we Indians hold about life in the United States and the personality that living their lifestyle creates. She looks good — healthy, with red hair and clothes that let us know that she is able to take care of herself. Her name is Georgia Quercia but, for me, this was always a difficulty — calling her by her name — because even though I came to know her well, she always retained this American perspective for me. It is hard for an Indian man, especially a low caste Indian man, to feel totally free of the vestiges of colonialism. This is not just my fault. They, too, the foreigners — the Americans in particular — seem to carry a notion of superiority. I feel what exists.

Memsahib, for example, insisted that she had heard of the phrase "fifty rupees for a penetration" before she came here and experienced what she did. Perhaps she had heard this. It had, after all, originated with the colonialists and even when the Indian says it, he says it in English. I don't know how it is said in Hindi or in Urdu. This phrase, it is always in English. This does not mean to say that the Indian man does not use prostitutes, he does but he uses a prostitute, rents a woman, in a distorted way now, one that is far away from a simpler exchange that was in place before the foreigners came.

Memsahib has also claimed that she knew of mandranioxide before she came to India, although she didn't know that this was the name. This is the American way, to know everything. She was no different in this respect. In the beginning, she was like any other tourist — just with a bigger agenda and good intentions — perhaps.

She trusted me in the end so that I came to know a side of her that revealed itself over time. It either revealed itself or it grew from nothing, but I like to believe that there was always a seed in Memsahib that, like me, knew how she connected to others so that Memsahib opened as she experienced India. She bloomed and became a real flower.

She had to have me to grow and she knew that I would understand better than any why she had changed. That is why she told me her side of the story.

One

The Four Hs: Honk, Henna, Hork, Honey

Georgia

I had pre-booked an airport hotel just outside of Mumbai,
and over a breakfast of peeled fruit and European croissants
— wonderstruck, culture-shocked, and a little scared — I ask
directions to get into Mumbai.

"No need for private transport, Miss. Take the Nine Bus to
the train station. Ask the driver. Say 'to Victoria, to Victoria
Station!' They will take you there, to the train station. The
train, it goes to Victoria Station. No problem, Memsahib."

Just standing in the heat and waiting for Bus Number Nine
is thrilling, despite my jet lag and the shoulder bag containing
three changes of clothes and a few necessities dragging my right
shoulder down. The buses pull in fast and I plan how to hop
on board, watching the Indians demonstrative jostling for space
and wondering if my white skin will give me an advantage. I'm
delighted as a dusty elephant hogs the centre of the equally
dusty road and causes bus number nine to stop long enough for
me to leap aboard. I say "Victoria, Victoria," as instructed, and
the driver gestures me to stay near him and then signals me off at
a train station. When I ask the man at the wicket which track I
should be on, using "Victoria, Victoria" once again, he points to
the train approaching and I puff up with pride at having gotten
it right, for it's all so foreign. But my self-assurance dwindles to
a trickle when I find myself in a boxcar rather than a coach and
realize that all of the occupants of the crowded car are standing
and all are men.

I squeeze my body against the wooden boxcar wall. I try to
be invisible, purposeful and confident as if I do this every day
but I sense that I'm a blinking white beacon that rivets every
eye. I can feel the attention prickling me like mosquito bites but
I know better than to scratch acknowledgement. The train is
stuffed and men hang from the handles on the doors to catch

the breeze. I maintain my centre and assume what I believe to be an immutable and unapproachable expression but my steely demeanour loses its polished patina when I see a train on the parallel tracks, overtaking this train, and am struck with the revelation that there are boxcars designated solely for females. Bright saris flutter past against the proverbial rusty wood of railway boxcar with the pretty commuters roosting and clucking in feminine seclusion. I use my luggage as a shield across my tummy and field the inquisitive stares of the male company at hand with a nonchalance darting with self-protection.

Once the train pulls into Victoria Station and I am free of the discrepancy, I regain my status, lift my chin high, and, exhilarated, head into the streets of Mumbai, clutching my belongings as I move through the pressing throng of early morning business. My ears are assaulted by honks. A mighty *hork!* of red beetle juice streams from the throat of a man with a briefcase and I barely sidestep the trajectory. My usually perfect henna bob is beginning to dissemble in the heat like runny honey.

My hotel, the City Palace, is cheap — thirty dollars, or one thousand and five hundred rupees. The clerk, with a dip into a dark inky hole, a shake of the wrist and hands, a wobbling head, and a smile of Indian welcome pens my information into a large, brown, leather-bound book, surely left over from the days of the British Empire. Names, passport numbers, countries of origin, planned itineraries — I join the list from the past and on the spot coin a private word, *nilt*, to describe this tilt-of-the-head-that-hasn't-direction combined with a-nod-that-isn't-a-yes that the clerk keeps doing each time that he looks expectantly in my direction. I sense that he is not really sure whether he has fulfilled his duties, but he has no need to worry, for I am charmed by the ornate formality of the very old lobby. He smiles again as he hands me the big caricatured key and I can see how much

he is eager to oblige; yet the wavering motion signals a hesitation of commitment when I ask for the time and he pulls out
a pocket watch. It's already ten and I'm meeting my guide at
eleven. Bernie's arranged it.

The man that Urban Help has recommended as my guide
sounds suitable. Bernie told me that he has talked at length
with our host research organization and with his brother-in-law,
Nur, and that they have assured him that Karma Pradesh will
serve as a bridge to the inner sanctums of the Indian sex trade.
Apparently he has connections and an inside track. I have
been told that he is both worldly and religious. I hope this isn't
Bernie's way of saying "straight and serious," because it has been
my experience that this is the type of person who finds it difficult
to accept me. We shall see.

Karma

I am Karma Pradesh and I am Indian. I was born in Mumbai. My
religion is Buddhist. My first language is Hindi. I am of no caste
because in India there is no caste system. Not in the New India
and I am a New Indian. They say this, that there is no caste, but I
was born low and although they say that I have the opportunity
to rise above the caste of my parents and achieve my goals, I am
not so sure. This is maybe true, maybe not so true — but I have
my way. The way I live my life is by following my Buddhist beliefs
and participating in my destiny.

I am thirty years old. I have not married. Marriage is of little
use to me, and since Indian women feel that it is of great use, I
have instead known women from other countries. I moved to
Goa from Mumbai with my mother when I was seven years old.
My mother had an accident and was horribly disfigured. Before
that, she was a beautiful woman, but she was also a prostitute. I
was a child raised in the company of many women with other

children like me, sometimes in school, and sometimes at home, for we also worked, the children of the women — washing, cooking, or looking after the younger children — but most of the time we were free. Then, I didn't know another way or another life and I was not unhappy. It was not until my mother's accident that I understood unhappiness. We moved to Goa when my mother was given in marriage to a man from Goa, a fisherman, and the man who I was made to call Father from that time was a man who was not my father.

If I initiate right actions, I will be rewarded. This is simple. It is the reasoning of karma. That my name is Karma and yet I am talking about karma may be difficult to understand. My culture can be very confusing for Western people but my name is Karma because Indian people believe in karma, destiny, and how it ties life together. My name reflects the ideas that are in my religion. My name tells others that I am a Buddhist and an Indian.

Karma is a way of living. I have been taught that I must respect my mother and my father, for they gave me the opportunity to live on earth as a man and that is already high on the ladder of beings. I am also responsible for the fact that I have been born into this life as a man. I was responsible for my karma before I was born into this life and I am responsible for my karma as I move through this life. I chose my father and my mother by doing actions in my last lives that made me into Karma today. There is a missing clue to my karma, for I do not know who is my real father and I do not understand why I am aligned with this man who is not my father but whom I must call father, or even to the woman who is my mother, my real mother, because I am not enlightened and I can only see this life, not my past or future lives.

I am the first child of seven, raised in one room, a beach house, a hut. Mother became a tired woman, too many births — seven in sixteen years is too many births. The new father, he is a drunk. He is a fisherman and a drunk. More a drunk than a fisherman. Too many nights in the darkness, this father sits drinking his *feni* liquor, staring at the Indian Ocean pounding on the seashells and swishing the fishnets. He sleeps days, sits nights, and when he was aroused, it happened, right there. In Mumbai, I saw men and women having sex; I heard them, as well, but not my mother. It is not a part of my memory, only the knowledge that came as I grew older. When I look on my history, since I was born into this life, there are many questions which I would like to ask. I would like to know what it is that is real and what I have believed is real. It is much the same when I consider my karma and question who I was in my past lives and how it is that who I was is now feeding my karma in my present life.

I do not know why I must call a drunk my father. Hindus, they are not usually drinking. This "father" is not a good Hindu, for his destiny is ruled by the lower chakras. He is like an animal with his needs stronger than his head. His lower energy centres rule his actions. His head does not shine with the light of understanding. I came through another man into this life and the reason why I came through him was to teach me a lesson, to show me something, as it is my destiny to know what it is to be his son. He left me with no clue, no idea who he was, and so his days, also, are filled with nothing from me, his son. He has none of the understanding of what it is to have me as his son.

I do not want to be like my second father. He is the drunk in a village of fishermen. He has never gone to school and he is also not even a fisherman. He can live in Goa because he received a dowry with my mother. Her dowry was large because she has many things wrong with her, and yet someone paid a big dowry to find her a husband. My mother was burned by battery acid when she came between two men fighting. This is why this man

who is not my father was paid to keep her for a wife. Her face
is scarred and she can't speak. She pushes the air from the back
of her throat and makes a noise like a faraway wind hitting the
sail of a Goan fishing boat, as if the air is trapped. The skin on
her face is wrinkled, pinched, and criss-crossed like the folds in
a lizard's skin where it is loose around its joints. She is not pretty,
but I remember at one time she had been pretty. My little sister
Dharma was pretty, and you could see Mother in her.

I remember the embarrassment in that hut, of listening to this
man who found it funny to wake me up when he came in late,
and then I would hear him with my mother, so I slept outside
on the beach or where I could, usually with the hippies. Later, in
more pleasant ways, with English girls, Dutch girls, French.

From that hut, four babies died. Dharma, my stepsister, was
the second child from my mother to live. She was born fourteen
years after me. Mother was over forty when Dharma was born
and after Dharma the genes in our family were polluted and
beauty stopped flowing into the children. Dharma was an angel
of goodness in our home, the candle that lit my family. Dharma
was the brightness, the only girl. Then beauty was replaced by
Down's syndrome, for the next two boys were damaged, and it
was then that this man called father stopped visiting our home
and slept out — except to interfere. On occasion.

Nunu, my stepbrother, was the first to show the signs. The
other boy, Durga, lies on a bench by the door most days. I have
heard it said that "father" carried a dirty seed. I knew that my own
beginnings did not contain any of this dirt but I worried about
whether Dharma escaped smudging. Indians use a smudge to put
the sweet smoke of incense into the home. It is many herbs tied
together with a string and when it is present the house is filled
with smoke and there is a beautiful smell. Down's syndrome is a
smudging of the mind and body that leaves behind only smoke,

no sweetness, only a sickly feeling that something has gone wrong. I am sorry for my brothers. Dharma, I thought, was different. She looked fine; always good-looking, not like our brothers, but she did not entirely escape the dirt that came through this other man who was not my father. It is a smudge on her karma that she received from her father. And the smoke from his smudge seeped in deep and killed her. I must become an action yogi in order to clear the air of the smoke from the smudge of the karma from my not-father's dirt.

I believe, for I am a Buddhist, that spirit is shaped by outlook. This creates karma. The experiences in a life and how those experiences are handled, that is a person's outlook. Even when I hated this new father, I believed that it was better to have a good outlook. In Goa, there are many foreigners who come to visit the Goan beaches. When I was a younger man, I liked the hippies, for they had an interest in our religion and a willingness to mix. I learned a lot from their ideas of freedom. They threw caste and status aside in favour of a less materialistic way of life. I, too, prefer a spiritual life, but I can also appreciate money, for I see that the materialistic life is also necessary. It is a fact of life. The hotels came to Goa and the simple life of the hippies, living in the old Goan homes left from the Portuguese, was no longer possible. And the hippies were too much with drugs. But I was never a hippie. I will not do drugs, even for spiritual reasons, like the saadhu. I am a modern Indian. I changed with the times. I am the blouse man. I know the way of making honest business.

I speak English and I read English. I understand German and French well enough to make business. I have had many businesses. I began by recycling the trash left by the hippies, the pop bottles and abandoned clothes, the stuff of the Westerners from knapsacks too heavy to carry. When I was fourteen, I began to work with a tailor, one who trusted me despite my youth, and

I began a blouse business. Before I had hair on my face, I became
"the blouse man."

I took full advantage of the Indian school system and
then after school I made friends with the foreigners who were
endeared by my baby sister, shyly tucked in behind me. I used
her sweetness to seduce the girls. My first sexual experience
was with a girl from Sweden. She had come to Goa wanting to
know more about our Indian way between spiritualism and sex.
Discipline is a part of the Buddhist way. A Buddhist must know
that if the body is disciplined, the mind will also be in shape. This
is the practice of yoga, a discipline to train the mind. In India,
you can practice sex in a spiritual life. This is the Tantra, where
sex helps to free the consciousness and move it to higher levels. I
was very young and thought that I would teach this Swedish girl
my youthful understanding of Tantric discipline, but she taught
me many more lessons.

The idea of nonattachment is a Buddhist way of dealing with
the suffering of life, but I learned this lesson best from a Swedish
girl. It was with great love that I knew her first, for she helped
me to understand that I could let love go and not be lost walking
the path of life. I have known many girls. They came to Goa and
then they went away. This was, for me, a good life.

My sister went to Mumbai to work as a domestic servant.
This is a great honour to work in the city and we were very
happy when our father said that he had arranged this for her.
When Dharma left, I was sad but happy for her, to know that she
would make money in the home of a rich family in Mumbai, an
Indian family.

But this is not what happened.

I am the one who is in Mumbai now. My mother sent me
here to find my little sister. I have learned many things here. It is
because of my sister Dharma that I am meeting with a woman

from America today at eleven. I am waiting for her and I am ready. She will help me to understand my path, my destiny, the action that is needed. The American woman and I have had a connection in an earlier life perhaps, or maybe this is the first time that we come together.

I will show this American woman what she wants to see. Urban Help has arranged for her to make the first of her discoveries this afternoon. We will see if this woman from America can look at this sex trade in India. It is not a pretty scene and I have found that the Western people have a difficult time with the part of India that is not beautiful. She is here to write a book. I will show her what she is looking for, but she will be showing me more than she suspects. Now I become a detective. I am no more the blouse man selling kurtas to tourists whose skin had burnt to the colour of a pomegranate. My path is different now that I have grown older.

Georgia

Karma Pradesh is extremely handsome, like the hand-painted cinema posters that I saw from the train. It's his smile, a little surly. He is dressed in a Western shirt and loose cotton pants, and because he has a natural elegance, his attitude as he sits, arm on the back of the simple bench, seems aristocratic. He nods slowly as he greets me.

"And if you are rested enough from your trip, I have arranged for you to meet a man I know, Memsahib. I help you find the sex trade in India and, if you are not too tired, we will begin the research right now. It is nasty business, Memsahib, and I am afraid you will not like what I show you."

"Your English is very good, Karma."

"Why not, Memsahib? I live in Goa and there are many English tourists who come to Goa. I go to school until I am sixteen years old, when I make a job selling shirts to the tourists. No problem, I am not a blouse man now, Memsahib. I work for Urban Help. If you are strong, we can soon go to the streets."

Karma is quick. I like that. Thank God he can speak English, for Mumbai is a raucous insistent *Honk!* with a muffled bleed-through from the past adding static to the present cacophony. There is background interference, as if the sound of an older India is on a station nearby; monkey chatter, the clatter of birds, the tweets and peeps of crickets, and the buzz of bees the size of badminton birds — *Kim*, Rudyard Kipling's perceptions, tuned in to this century. It is overwhelmingly present and yet soaked in something so far away from what I know that Karma's simple English vocabulary is a respite in the midst of it all.

"I take you to see a famous — bad famous — pimp. His name is Gurda. Gurda is in trouble, and Urban Help, they know Gurda. It's a long story, Memsahib. I tell you another time. Gurda, he owes a favour to Urban Help. He is a man who is a little afraid of trouble, but this time, no problem, Memsahib, he will help you to see a prostitute — in action!

"I am not a bad man and please do not think that I am because I show to you bad actions, bad men. I want good karma, good actions. When I make good actions, the good karma follows. In my life now there is a shame. I must fix my karma. I am on a path, Memsahib, and you are on a path, two paths, like this — crossing! So many stories, Memsahib. We help, you and me, together."

Karma sets an energetic pace. We walk through a series of small streets and end up in a crowd of men in Western suits who are gathered around a food stall in front of a large modern building with bronze letters showing that it is The Mumbai Stock Exchange. Karma elbows through to where a vendor flicks pancakes from griddle to palm. There are robed, wigged men — they look like judges — amongst the businessmen pushing close to his wagon. There are not many women and those that I see are in the traditional Indian dress. Standing off to one side, a man with a strawberry birthmark on the right side of his face squarely meets my eyes as he greets Karma. He speaks Indian to Karma, but he never takes his eyes off me as if he is engaged in a face-off where he knows the rules and is attempting to communicate them to me by locking me into his game. I do not like this man, immediately. There is something too "out there," as if he is too foreign to ever be able to relate to.

Karma doesn't extend the courtesy of introducing him to me and I can sense that I am best kept aloof. Gurda has caramel whites surrounding reddish brown irises with pinpoints for pupils. He smells sickly sweet and I don't know why but I am further repulsed by this man when I see his eyes, as if a sense awakened by his proximity and heightened by the heat and the sweat has tapped into a stream in my subconscious that I wish to forget. As he speaks to Karma, I sense that I have been brought here as a witness to their transaction but I can feel that this pimp doesn't like my being here. His glare burns into me like a lit cigarette pressed into skin. When he breaks his aggressive glare, he leaves abruptly, blending into the murk of beige that hangs on the periphery of the nobler lunch crowd.

Karma steers me closer to the stall and asks for two masala dosas.

"Ten rupee, Memsahib. I pay, Memsahib. Expense account. You know this, 'expense account'? Look, now, at man rolling dosa. His name is Rani."

Karma lays a line of chutney on the fat dosa and with a series of neat bites he finishes off one of the stuffed pancakes. He backs through the small crowd that has gathered around me. He shields me as we walk back to the hotel, explaining that the vendor where we got the food, Rani, will pay for the services of a prostitute who Gurda, the pimp, will have riding in a boxcar that we will be hidden in.

"The commuter prostitute is from far away. She have a pimp to find men. Her pimp is Gurda. Tonight we meet Dahli. She is coming from south — Goa. I, too, my home is Goa, so we talk the same. Gurda, he pimp Dahli many times. You watch tonight, Memsahib. I meet you — twenty hours. We go in rickshaw to train station. I have paid the train man. We go into boxcar seven. We hide behind *coir*, Indian rope. There is big size, big round like this, rope in boxcar seven. That is the reason we say seven boxcar — good hide-in place.

"Rani, the masala dosa vendor, he wants commuter whore. Rani is the dosa man. Got it straight? Lot of confusion, Indian names, Memsahib. Rani and Gurda. This is my special interest. I have special interest."

Karma distances and grows quiet. I'm glad, for he's very intense and this has all been conducted in a heat that is overwhelming. His face narrows to a determined furrow of concentration. He shows me the door into the City Palace Hotel.

"Eight o'clock, Memsahib. We meet here. We have a date!"

Karma seems capable but tonight is more than I had expected — a first encounter, arranged by Urban Help. I hope I'm up to it. It seems a dangerous venture and that pimp, Gurda, what a thoroughly disgusting man. A weasel. Or a lizard, from the lizard people that Bernie talks about.

My room in the City Palace Hotel is quiet once I close the shutters, the ceiling fan keeping it cool. I slip into domesticity, arrange for the laundry service offered by the hotel to pick up a small bundle of clothes. I write, and enjoy a pot of chai brought to my room. I feel refreshed and venture out to find an email outlet to send a message back to Bernie letting him know that I've arrived and made contact.

"Fifty rupees for a penetration!"

There it was! Gurda, the pimp, shouts the words out of the door of the train as it starts to slowly move out at the second stop from Victoria Station. In English! One barking signal and then he ducks back into the car where Karma and I are hidden in the dark. I see Karma's black eyes widen and tense as Gurda calls out, so that the white circles around his irises seem to turn on like a fluorescent light, almost to the point of signalling our stealthy presence. Positioned to watch from the dark corner of the railway boxcar, we are standing behind the piles of rope. The four of us — Gurda the pimp, the prostitute who is called "Dolly," Karma, and myself — had been quickly handed onto the train by a plump conductor. The prostitute is not easy to see from here and I'm sure she is making it that way. She seems shy. One of her hands is missing digits — her first finger and thumb. She had it folded under her other hand but I saw when she used the door handle to pull herself up onto the boxcar platform. I suppose this is an extremely unusual situation for her, to know that I am here, watching her. Apparently, we will talk with her later.

As we pull out, I spot him. Rani, running alongside the train. Rani, with the sweat dripping from the exertion and probably generations of malnutrition, has made his appointment. He had been told to board the commuter train as dusk turned to darkness and it slowed down at the second station from Mumbai. He is on time. I am as excited as if I was waiting for a first date, sexually heightened in much the same way, expectant, eager, perversely curious, but I am also physically unsettled by motion sickness and feel my breathing is stifled.

Rani appears to be having trouble getting in. In the moon-light illuminating the open door Gurda catches the wrist of the gaunt, panting man and levers him up and onto the boxcar platform so that, as he enters, Rani dramatically turns to face into the shadowy recesses. Although I know he can't see us, for the coils of Indian coir piled in the back like big shaggy dogs are adequate protection, I feel conspicuous, as if my whiteness is a pulsing night light.

"Fifty rupees for a penetration!" Gurda tugs on Rani's cotton shirt sleeve in order to position him away from our corner. Rani's attention is drawn to the dark-skinned girl, who is standing, as if coy, behind the flesh-broker.

Karma whispers and I start at his closeness. "Watch. Bargain."

A perky nipple presses against the frayed fabric of the dark whore's dress like a hidden raspberry inviting the john to partake in her confection. Rani, leering, twitches from foot to foot as the train car clickety-clacks through the shanty suburbs. I can tell that he is playing it cool as he haggles with Gurda and makes as if to jump off the train again.

Gurda is hanging out the door of the open boxcar with the wind in his hair. He looks liberated and confident; a strange aura of ease has come over him. The pose seems to be granting him a sense of freedom and he is chuckling through the bargaining, as if he is enjoying himself. I can see that Rani is madly impatient through Gurda's display of petty power, so he decides to go for it, counting out five ten-rupee notes and handing them over to Gurda, who adds to their patina as he hides them in the stained rolled waist of his dhoti.

The dark-skinned prostitute looks away from Rani's dirty grin and draws her dress up. I hear her back crunch against the boxcar boards. She directs her gaze off into the recesses of the boxcar as if distancing herself and she starts with surprise as our eyes meet. Her widening eyes appear to mirror my own tension as they expand like Karma's had a moment ago. The luminous white appears to obliterate the dark brown of her irises as the expansion of her pupils overwhelms them.

I am not ashamed to watch. I stare back and I am in awe of her. I see her accepting this man who is somewhat rough with her and oblique, as if he is the one ashamed, and yet she is almost radiant. She shivers, raises her forefinger to her lips and with a nod of her head gestures at me to be silent. I am fully present in the intensity of the instant as I comply.

Twelve to sixteen strokes and Rani withdraws — done. The woman lets the simple housedress slip back over her knees. Gurda takes out the bundle of money to count his fee as he barks again, "fifty rupees for a penetration!" into the dark recesses of the boxcar, seemingly just for the effect; but I start as I recognize a silhouette in the door from the next carriage. As the figure moves forward with a male swagger, the trio — the john, the pimp, and the prostitute — are busted by the blinding flashlight of the fat conductor who had helped us aboard the train. With sleazy deference Gurda moves away from the woman, as if he has nothing to do with her. The conductor is authoritarian with a command issued, and to syncopated metal-on-metal of wheels on track, Rani holds her from behind.

"Bad times," Karma whispers, and his closeness is too close, for this second encounter is too intimate, too abusive, a shock. I see that we have somehow lost control of this febrile experiment and embarrassment is setting into me as the conductor quickly unloads his frustrations, pumping into the woman so hard that she cries at each penetration. Then Rani, as he is watching the conductor thrust, grows visibly hard once again. I have lost the anchor of the prostitute's gaze and, stranded in inaction, I cringe as the conductor, tension released, holds her for Rani and I see him humping her again.

The mess at the end of all the sex is excruciating. The smell of cum is sickening. The distressed woman has turned away from us to clean herself and there is an incomprehensible chatter of protest as she arranges herself. Gurda is engaging in a bullying inept attempt at excusing himself. The conductor brusquely exits and Rani is all swagger and bravado. Much can be understood when the actions are so physically blatant; the raised shaking fist, the whispers screeching, the swat of the woman's hand at the pimp.

When Rani leaps from the boxcar, we move. I am sheepishly shaken and can't maintain my balance with the rush of the train, so that I lurch into an awkward stumble. I find myself on my knees before the prostitute, who breaks what I comprehend to be the men's hesitation to touch a white woman and, dropping reserve, she gives me a hand up. I shiver to the next stop, where the four of us get off. Then, once Gurda has left, we bring Dolly back with us to the restaurant below my hotel.

I feel horrible. I am so sorry for this poor woman. That boxcar. That was far beyond those sex clubs in New York. That was everything low imaginable.

This poor woman. Under the strip lights, I see her now. She is young, with some kind of white powder on her face that make her eyes look bright black, but it has become patchy with sweat. Her mutilated right hand makes me think at first that she may have been a thalidomide baby, although I can't imagine that the deforming drug could have been given to lower-class Indian women. And then the right or wrongness of my research pops out again and I remember what I just watched.

I try to focus outward on this woman across the table from me. I see that she's accustomed to keeping her hand hidden and

I don't get a good look before she's slipped it back onto her lap. Then I backtrack into shame at my curiosity once again. Do I see people only as feeding my own use? What did I just watch? What is her name again? — Dolly, Karma said she was Dolly. As she drinks her tea, she brings her hand up to hold the glass with her bad hand — the right hand, the "eating" hand in India, where the left is used for cleaning — cupping the right with the left held in front, not touching it, thus preventing inspection. As Karma starts translating what she is saying, I am forced from speculation into attention. The evil spell still lingering from the train breaks — not apart but open — as her story is told.

I understand from his translation that Dahli (Karma spells it for me) had been at the end of her tether. She has a little girl whom she leaves wherever she lives when she rides the trains for tricks. Tonight, she had been given the chance to get clear of the sex trade. Yet there seems to be a certain amount of par-for-the-course in her story. She appears somewhat stupid with her nonchalance and I wonder why she had appeared radiant to me. Tonight, pimped by Gurda, she had lifted her dress to receive the stinking excretions of a twitching worker from Mumbai. Probably not unusual. But tonight there were others involved in the evening's comings and goings, for trouble had indeed entered when they had been intercepted by the conductor. Dahli had been put through more than was bargained for. She tells Karma that as the first man held her arms behind her back, with the train worker unbuckling his pants in a fervour — she mimes out his frenzy — she could still see that this was the end and that she had to continue. She says that she was already a part of our side, an upside as she describes it, one that has a movement that is progressing upward rather than regressing into the darkness. I *had* seen it in her shining eyes but then she had suffered another and then yet another penetration as that foul-smelling Rani had used her again. She tells us that she knows without doubt that this was the last time she would be used like that. She says that she knows she is on the path to her freedom and as she talks she seems more elevated than I. I, who was motivated to watch by what? By a book contract. I listen like a zombie, more in a dead realm than present.

Finally, Karma says he will take Dahli in a rickshaw to her home. He tells me to wait until tomorrow and he will be able to tell me her story in more detail.

I don't need the prompting. I am exhausted beyond words.

Karma

Dahli is from a different part of Goa than I am but it is good to talk in our language. She tells me that she was a Christian but that she is no longer sure and I tell her that I am a Buddhist but that my mother was a Hindu, and we are both Indians from Goa so that we know a life that is similar. She is rough from her life and I listen more than I speak on the long rickshaw ride.

"In Mumbai, I found a paper — Urban Help. I kept it many months. I do not always like to be a prostitute but I didn't know how to stop the flow of my life. I was afraid to stop. But something happened to me. I thought of how far away I had come from myself. I used to be pretty, happy, full of love and life. But now I am old and fat and I am only twenty-four years and the man who brought me to Mumbai — he is Moona — is not a part of my life now. And I have a little girl who is more like me than I am like me. She is more like me when I was pretty and happy and I do not want to see her grow older here, for I know what they do here. She will grow older than me very fast if they have their way.

"Would you like to hear my story? I have not been a saint."

I tell Dahli that my story, too, has a blow of shame upon my karma and the karma of my family. I say to her, "Yes, tell me your story and I will listen, for I want to know about the man who is the father of your child."

I tell her, "I am an adult, Dahli. I know the ways of the world. Tell me, just once, the story of Dahli, and then let's look only to the future. No more of where we have been. Only the path forward."

Dahli hesitates, then begins. "It was in the dark church in Goa — do you know this church, the Basilica of Bom Jesus in Old Goa? — that I first learned about sex, not from boys, but from Sister Agnes, a holy woman, my teacher in school. I was to help her. When you are a student in the Christian school, you sometimes help the teacher. I was teacher's assistant for Sister Agnes. I was a good student. Smart. She told me that I was given this honour because I know how to think and I can imagine many things.

"One afternoon, after class, Sister Agnes told me the story of her namesake. Would you like to hear it?"

I urge her on, for I am after the knowledge that will change my karma.

"Agnes was a beautiful, chaste woman, very young, who had pledged her life to be the bride of Jesus Christ. She lived only for the day when she could enter the nunnery and live a life of service to her Lord Jesus. Her beauty, however, was so extraordinary that she attracted the notice of a very rich man. Her family was poor and the rich man was her father's boss. The rich man begged her father for the hand of his daughter, but he was told that the girl wanted to be a nun. The rich man insisted. Agnes said no, again and again. So, do you know what the rich man did?"

Dahli is a strange combination. She is very trusting, almost childlike as she talks. But there is also a roughness. She directs the rickshaw driver every now and then with a tap on his shoulder and a direction. It is a maze of small streets in this part of Mumbai.

"He cut off her breasts!"

She seems to relish the horror, so I respond with my reaction of horror.

"Yes, very horrible! And I was very young when Sister Agnes told me this story. I was shocked. And then Sister Agnes asked me if I had breasts yet. More shock to hear my teacher ask me this! And this is when it began. Sister Agnes finished the tale of Saint Agnes with the sad image of her death upon a hot bed of coals — this was arranged by the same rich man — but before the story had ended, Sister Agnes's hands ..."

Dahli is not telling me the right part of her life. I want to know about Moona, the father of her daughter. It is Moona who is important to us, so I try to shift the story, but she is not listening. She wants to tell me *her* story. I must let go of my direction, the path that I want to take toward Moona, and listen to her again. Her story, still, shows my path forward and I see also that she needs help. She is hurt, this talkative woman with the dark skin of the southern people and the twisted hand.

"Yes, Sister Agnes, a Portuguese nun with white skin — yet always she looked bad, a little mean or unhappy — was the one who showed me how to find God within my own body. Sister Agnes awoke my sleeping heaven. And Sister Agnes liked to open me to the light as we kneeled in prayer in the dark empty chapel before a very beautiful statue of Christ. The wood of Christ was polished by my father — he made the statues and polished the warm wood to the softness of skin. The head of Our Lord hung over and there was a shadow because his hair was long and he had a horrible crown — of thorns! To me, it seemed more a brown skin than a white man's face — Jesus was a white man — and the eyes glowed. I remember that, and underneath the cloth, Jesus was round and smooth, like a woman! Sister Agnes lifted Jesus's cloth in order to show me."

Dahli pauses. She wiggles as if she is sitting on something too hard. She stops to frown, to pout. I am relieved. This story is intense.

"I did not tell you this — I had no mother. She died when she gave me life. I loved Sister Agnes. I cried when Sister Agnes left the church and moved away from the basilica. You may think that all of this was wrong, but for me it wasn't. I was young, true, but I liked Sister Agnes and also I loved her. I loved Sister Agnes. And I like sex. I really do like sex. But I lost my happiness until I met Moona — Moona, with his slim body and heavy-lidded eyes. Moona was like the polished wooden Christ. And Moona was my saviour. I was almost too ready for him, this man from Mumbai who had the body of my Christ. I remember when he first removed the light cotton dhoti that covered him. He said, 'Touch it, it's like velvet.'"

Dahli inhales, for she has been talking very fast. She is breathless, but she assures me, "Yes, you will meet Moona tomorrow. I know what I am to do for you and I am prepared to do this. But I cannot wipe out my history. When Moona found me, I was no longer at the basilica and I was very sick. I had lost my thumb and my finger at the cashew factory … but this is a different story. But we loved, truly, and Moona knew a gentler life for a very small time. Not for long, only as far as Maria's birth, and then maybe one year. We are coming close to my home and I must tell you the rest another time."

Dahli is silent now. Her face is actually quite lovely when she stops talking, although she looks swollen around the eyes. Her neck is thick and she is right, she is older than her years. But her lips are full and sensual, and I can see how she must have been beautiful when she was younger. I wonder how old she was when Moona took her away.

She causes me to start with her sudden vehemence.

"Help me do it! I'll bring Maria, my daughter, and start life new. She can go to school at Urban Help, can't she? They have told me. They have schools. It is true, please. It is true? Help me find the love and protection of Jesus Christ by living a good life. I am afraid, for I do not know who I am betraying. Do I betray the father of my little girl, the man who gave her life, the man I love still? Moona was tired by my unhappiness, you see. He wanted to get rid of me. He was thinking business, the son of his father. Moona is from Dilly Willy. He was more from Dilly Willy than from a polished warm wooden statue. He betrayed me, sold me, again and again he sold me!"

Of Jesus Christ, I know little. The Christians have strange stories. I prefer the simple stories of the Buddhist way. I believe that Dahli is crippled, not so much in her hand as in her spirit, and I hope that we can trust this American woman to help us. Dahli is Indian like me even if she is Christian. Tonight we live in India, changing our karma, making Indian business.

Dahli tells the rickshaw to stop. I hate these areas, these city slums. I prefer the beach houses to these Mumbai slums — shacks made of cardboard and tin. And her little girl is here. I give her shoulder a small pat as we arrange to meet tomorrow, but I am glad to see her go. This is a rotting life she is living.

Poor woman.

As her feet touch down on the dusty ground, they stir a cloud of warm powdered earth. It is comforting. It is India. And it was the same in Goa, these dusty clouds at each footfall.

Georgia

It may have been the heat or it may have been the pause-and-go way of having to listen as Karma translated Dahli's words, but I am not able to connect to this experience with any sense of realism. I am unable to ground even though I am back here, in my space, my room. I am awash on a rugged raft in a sea where the waves have me on the verge of vomiting. I am more at sea than on this nice clean bed in the City Palace Hotel. India and this sudden initial shocking experience make me wonder if I have stepped in over my head.

The face of that poor woman as she was talking, with the powder still dappled on her cheeks! I wanted to tell her to look in her mirror, in *my* mirror, to see what she looked like, but I could see on her face that she was also studying me, sizing me up, looking at me, with her attempt to identify with me as strange as mine was with her.

She said that in the beginning she had been afraid to do what she had been asked to do in front of a white woman but that she knew that this was a penetration — this word used for sex is so abrupt! — that would release her. She got quite excited, and I realize now that what I had first taken to be stupidity might have been pride. She made a step tonight that was hard for her to take. It was elation that I saw when our eyes connected in the boxcar. It was her knowing what was happening and looking over and seeing me only shocked without seeing rejection. She believes I can help her. This helps me settle down. This thought that something might be getting better.

But I *still* can't see why it had all happened. Surely this hasn't been for my benefit only, to show me that there is a story to be told here. What have I started?

Nothing. I am not that important. I arrived in the middle of this woman's story. It was her life that I saw changing tonight, not mine.

Two

Cacophonic Circus

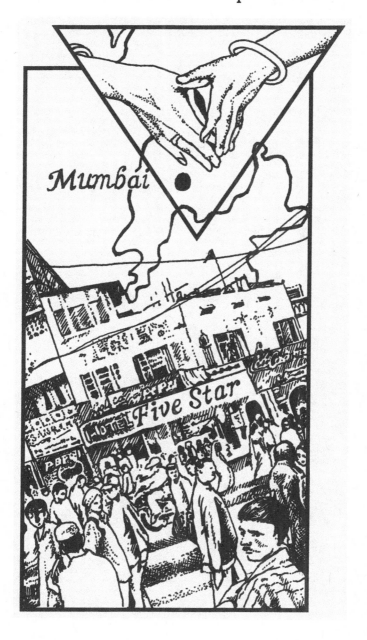

Georgia

A good night's sleep seems impossible here, a Western fiction. There is so much noise, extraneous information thrusting in through my dreams. I woke myself up with slow muffled moaning, trying to surface from the scariness. I had dreamt that I was in a place dark and dangerous. I was dodging, trying to be invisible, hiding, under cover. Then I began to feel hands on me. I struggled free by willing myself to rise higher, above the grave call of the heavy dream.

I take a walk, waiting for the hour when I am to meet Karma at the restaurant. I yield to the immediate, trying to be all eyes and less mind. It is from my head that I am susceptible to falling down, when I ramble to places where I am insecure, where I am unable to find a tangible focus. I will force myself to be *here*. It is my best chance to feel sane, the surest source of insight, to be present here in Mumbai, this city that is all decorated, dyed, and embroidered like a welcome flag.

And as I will it, so it happens, and I begin to see what is around me. Henna graces the beard of a fumbling old man whose white hair, coarse and damaged, provides the perfect field of frayed stems to soak up the red dye. Bindis made of *kumkum* powder dot foreheads. A green sari is matched with a spot of phthalo green powder, a red with cadmium, an orange with ochre, a blue with cobalt, much as accessorizing with a purse, earrings, or shoes. Kohl, a greasy black eyeliner made from charcoal, which is dabbed on the finger and then drawn between the eyelids with one fast swipe, protects the eyes from flies as it beautifies an Indian man's inherently sultry look. He twirls his moustache as he passes by, watching me as if assessing some foreign material for necessary flaws. Deep red gobs of pan, a mixture of herbs and spices wrapped in a betel leaf and chewed as a mild stimulant, sprinkle the dust, broken stones, and pitted pavement like bloodstains, glistening or caked, as if offering up remnants of a murder scene.

As I walk, beggars cluster, their hands a flurry of intrusive demands that make me uncomfortable in the face of their stilted English — a meagre, utilitarian vocabulary. And their smell. They smell like warm tomato soup. They are a launching pad for flies and moving, twinkling dots can be seen in the dark strands of the children's matted hair. I find it hard to figure out what might be the formula for ridding my pangs of conscience — a pocket of change, one, two or five rupees? — but the beggars swarm me and I react as if I am allergic to bees as I block their stinging demands. The need of the poor is palpable. It's crawling across them, a drab, dusty shade of cow dung, colouring them beige and draining down a sludge pipe. I am sucked into their pathos and hand over a fistful of soiled rupees.

Karma

Near to the City Palace Hotel, Memsahib's high-class hotel above the vegetarian restaurant, there is another hotel — Hotel Five Star — with rooms to rent for one hundred and fifty rupees. This is the hotel where Gurda brings the new prostitutes before they are turned over to Dilly Willy, who is the Grand Beggar and Whore Master, a man who is feared and known even far away from Mumbai. There is one new girl here now, soon to be deflowered. It is not, sadly, the usual preparation before a wedding. It is a horrible preparation, with Gurda soliciting for men to take the little bird by surprise.

Last night on the train was difficult for me, but there was a lesson in being at this encounter. My sister Dharma did not have a long struggle. She did not live long as a prostitute. She would have been like Dahli if she had been used for years as Dahli was used. Dahli is like the masala dosa. Her experiences have affected her. Now, she is spiced very hot and she may be a long time with the scent of this strong spice. I do not like this strong smell, but Dahli is important to Urban Help and Urban Help is important to change the karma that has affected my sister and caused her death. It is a mutual exchange, for Urban Help can alter Dahli's karma as well and then she will not smell so strongly. Dahli was brought to the train so that I could meet her and soon meet Moona. And we use the American woman, too. We are forming a karmic map. We are explorers charting the land as we go. We begin on high mountains of consciousness, frightening peaks of knowledge, and then follow the river that flows to the sea and joins the waters of other rivers. In the sea, the future will reveal the truth of the past as deceptions are washed away.

We are all connected together. Many people think of karma in terms of an amazing and special moment of destiny rather than a path in which all events participate to form a new way of being. We Indians understand the idea of series. This is the Indian way to the workings of destiny. The Buddhist word for this series of karmic events is *dharma*. Dharma — the name of my sister. Dharma is law. It is not a dead law, but a living law, as one action affects another. Our lives twist together, balance — and that is the dharma.

Last night, many lives wove together to make knowledge. Even if the knowledge is frightening or evil, we are too small to understand why we are given the knowledge. I do not know why I was given the karma that I have. My sister died and now my life joins with more people to understand this karmic act. I am a young man and I am an Indian man, so I see with Indian eyes, eyes with the dark stain of kohl around the rims.

Last night was the first step on a twisting path that will join more people together to create a new way of being. I do not know what this new form of being is until I am there, but I know that it will come, will happen, will become, because it will have a past and a future being contained within it.

I had never met Dahli before last night and I did not at first understand why I was to meet her, but now I know better. She is coming free from the sex trade. She will have a new law, new rules, a new form of being, because her special past brought her to the possibilities that last night makes for her today. Rebirth does not only happen when we die, but many times during our life we are reincarnated. It is not so simple, but also not so complex. This is a trade, like business. When I was the blouse man, I would trade rupees for cloth and the service of a tailor. There were ways that we did business, like a game that we were playing on both sides. Urban Help is trading Dahli's support for information because the father to Dahli's child is Moona, and Moona is Dilly Willy's son. She will introduce me to Moona and this will bring me to Dilly Willy. Today, I will see Dilly Willy, the man who is responsible for Dharma's death. I will not lose his face. It will not disappear although there are many faces in my head. I will remember Dilly Willy.

And Memsahib will again be a witness, at least for a part of today. We will see if she has the courage. She was scared last night. I could see this. She fell. Dahli was upset to touch her but she was not embarrassed by her. I did not want to touch her. She is not like the other white women I have known for pleasure and Tantric acts. I think that we are like bugs to her. We are her "research."

My sister Dharma died in a brothel in Pune. It will be the first destination on our trip, where I will introduce the American woman to Nur, from Urban Help. But first, I am going to use my time in Mumbai to come as close to Dilly Willy as I dare.

I want to kill this man.

I have a sick job this morning, for I will be walking the path that my dear sister was forced upon when she came to Mumbai.

Gurda is a fool. He has bragged when he should have remained silent; he has invited me to see the new girl. He tells me that she is still a virgin. He briefs me as we walk up the sloping stairway, narrow and slipping to the left so that I must hold my body away from the wall as I follow his dirty back to the third floor. He is a pitiful man, caught by his little ideas of importance, but he is also dangerous and nasty. Last night's encounter seems to follow him, wafting down to hang heavy over my head. I steel myself and call upon Maha Kali, the warrior, for protection against his energy. I dread seeing this new girl, this virgin, and although we have climbed only two floors in this typical Indian hotel, I am tiring on this broken stairway that throws me into the wall. There are no foreign tourists here. Not even hippies can find these places.

Gurda has been cool to me this morning. No greeting, only a piercing locking of eyes as if he is trying to hypnotize me into doing what he wants. I am short with him, disgusted, but I want to learn where I can see the man who is the king of evil, and if it is through this stupid man that I come to see Dilly Willy, I can play my part.

"Laxmi is the name of the new girl. Later today, when her virginity is gone, I will take the girl to the main brothel at the stables. Dilly Willy — man of many business — is main man. Dilly Willy is in control of prostitution, beggars, transportation, main time horse business. Rickshaws and buggies. Dilly Willy. Har! Horses and women, the same. Both are nothing to him, small specks of dirt. Today, I will show him Laxmi, twelve years, no longer a virgin by the time he gets a look at her!"

I am made sick by Gurda, and when he turns to look directly at me, because he is above me on the stairs, he is higher than me; but he is a small man to me, a man of small stature. As he searches my face, I see that he wants me to like him. He is trying to see if I am *really* with him, and I return his look with such convincing malice that he becomes confused, embarrassed, turns away and babbles on.

"Men like a virgin...."

Gurda has stopped outside an old door with paint chipped, grimy from the smoke of cooking, lamps, and general city pollution.

"It is sick job, but I have family." Gurda talks on like a girl talks too much. "Agrani will be first man. Very important man, government job. He like virgins. Agrani? He like this ..." Gurda holds up his wrist and a stained circle of thumb and forefinger. "And fat, like this ..." and he stares down my widening glare as he turns the key in the padlock and lifts the door so that it doesn't scrape on the wooden floor.

The shutters are closed and it's dark inside, but I see her crumpled on the straw mat. I am hit by the sight of a child dreaming with a visible jerky intake and exhalation of breath. I think of my sister who was small and downy-skinned like this girl, a sweet and sensitive girl, my sister, full of a brimming desire to please. And now she is dead. She has been dead for too long. She had entered the bardo state long before I discovered she was dead. I could not help her through the bardos. I could not do puja.

Gurda has shut up. He, too, stares down at the girl. We are caught in the same filthy realm and I feel sickened by the inevitable.

The girl's thumb is close to her mouth, pointing toward the tip of a tiny tongue. She trembles as she breathes as if she is a puppy having a bad dream. Her arm shelters her head and her right leg is drawn up. Her back is exposed. Sleeping on her tummy — she looks even younger than her vulnerable twelve years. Dharma was thirteen. A child. I look over at Gurda, who shrugs and shudders, breaks and acts. He draws the door shut, not forgetting to relock it on his sleeping catch, and whispers to

me to follow him out to a tenuous balcony where the racket of
Mumbai claps like the warning before a lightning strike.

Gurda perches his skinniness on a railing and lights a *bidi*,
twirling the tobacco twisted in a betel leaf so that his fingers stain
the pink thread wrapped around the dried brown leaf. He coughs
between drags as his raspy voice, scarred by years of inhaling
Mumbai's exhaust, begins to unload with a whining croak. I am
glad he is babbling on, for I am struck dumb by the thunderous
sight of the sleeping virgin child.

Gurda hacks out a gawky laugh. "My family? I say, 'I work at
a road job,' I tell them 'I can't live at home.' They believe me. They
want to eat. Hard times, you know, hard times...."

He blows a ring of smoke above the tangle of wires that loop
from balcony to balcony and he scratches his itches like a dog
jumpy with fleas.

"I get the girls. Big job, my job! Important job. Difficult job.
Hard times with the police, big jokes, ID stamped all the same.
'Laxmi, domestic worker.' All the girls the same — domestic
worker! Police, big jokes, like prostitutes. Important! Government,
rupees, top to bottom and bottom to top, rupees up, rupees down.
No lie, Karma! You meet me later, I show you."

The story has Gurda's head wagging and reinforces my creeping suspicion that Gurda may have an opium habit and be due
for the normalizing effects of the calming drug. He complains
and yet boasts on, as if the repetition of practicalities is a mantra
to drone out the consequences of his job. We are riveted in this
steely corner where our paths have jutted together. And as Gurda,
steeped in the sense of his life, drops deeper into a backwater, it
releases me from our lock.

He appears to have drowned, a lost man, but from somewhere
he makes a twisted acrobatic leap back up for air and continues.
"I take girl to Dilly Willy later today. My job. I take girl cured

— crack coconut, pop papaya, spice masala dosa — then Dilly
Willy give me the money and I done…. Until the next girl…."

Gurda unloads, like shit, a story of Mumbai. I lose my centre
and bark, like a dog, at his bragging, and yet it sucks him in to his
insecurity; he wants me to like him, so that he tells me an address
where I should meet him at 18:00 where I will see the great Dilly
Willy himself.

"No worry, Karma, my man. I protect you. Meet me, no
worry."

Gurda's stomach pulls in like a blow has been delivered and
he moves back a step and I see that something dangerous has
just happened. Something has tipped. Perhaps Gurda had felt a
peculiar safety in unloading his feelings before me, hypnotized
by the possibilities that lie behind new eyes and my association
with the white American. I see he is confused and I realize he is
playing both sides and has lost a clear idea of which side I am on.

And as the sugary smell of opium drifts across the balcony,
Gurda excuses himself, a flesh dealer, a small man, to meet the
beckoning finger of opiate forgiveness, and in his leaving I can
see he is as dull as to almost fade away. He retreats to a dark room
where eyes of opium close over a dream, the black drug heavy
on the lids.

But I cannot dull my pain. I know too much sadness. My
mind knows too much pain. And it is my karma now to know
that there is a child behind the closed door and I feel like I should
be reporting this to someone before it happens. But to who? I
would not see the face of Dilly Willy if I was to stop this flow of
flesh. Destiny does not always unfold as we would like it and I am
tied in to a chain of actions and reactions.

I will tell Memsahib. It is strange how we Indians need the
Western people. This is an Indian problem. Indian karma. My
karma is between a not-father and a not-son, for a sister from her

brother. This American woman, Memsahib, can do nothing. She can serve only as a witness and she can help by knowing and then relaying the news elsewhere; but she cannot help this girl, Laxmi, here and now. It is already too late and Memsahib is not Indian. She has no power for today.

The day after tomorrow when we are in Pune, Memsahib will know the story of my sister. This is the path that my sister travelled. But before she hears the story of my sister, Memsahib will know this story. She needs to listen to this story of the little girl Laxmi.

They underestimate us, the Western people. It is because of language. They think that because I am not speaking to them as clearly as they speak to each other, that I know less. But I am also privileged. I cannot say it as clearly as she would like and she cannot hear what I have to say with clarity, for she is not Indian. I see Memsahib struggling to understand, but she is the one who is creating the difference. I am the same as her but I understand that it is my karma to see this circle of events and yet perhaps not understand at all.

We meet again in the veg restaurant. Early afternoon. It is busy with Indians and a few tourists. Memsahib looks as bright as a new student and brightens even more when I tell her that we are off on a small mission. I am bringing her to meet Moona today.

But first, now that I know, I begin. "Gurda told me a story, Memsahib. This is not a good story. A girl — twelve-year-old girl — I not so sure, Memsahib, you okay, to listen?"

My knowledge of Laxmi is hurting me. It is too close to me. The inside of my head is straining toward my scalp. I am embarrassed about this sordid wisdom.

Memsahib tells me again that her name is Georgia, and she tries to reassure me that it is all right to call her this, but it is unreal. She is far away from this business and I tell her that for now I must call her Memsahib because she is from a different world than I am from. I can see that this disappoints her. She thinks she is strong, but she is open in her emotions and I can see that she is having trouble to keep up.

"You can tell me this story that you want to tell me, Karma. It is by others knowing that the bad things will be stopped eventually. It is the reason why I am here, Karma — to make things better."

The reason you are here, Memsahib, is to change the dharma, and as she voices her words of reassurance, I doubt her more. India is a puzzle that she is now living. India has many layers. She will never see a clear picture. It is for her a foreign puzzle, an Indian puzzle.

I am careful with my story. I tell her the girl's name. This is important for me, that she knows the name. I let her know that she is being held prisoner and that the hotel is nearby, so that she can see that she is very close to this world that she has said she wants to know. When I tell her that it was right here in the veg restaurant that Gurda recruited the men who will break her virginity, she peers around as if she can tell who might have been the culprits. But there will be many men who give Gurda money; like bidding at market — there is a deal. I let her know that it is important to see blood because the Indians are afraid of AIDS and the men think they will be safe from AIDS if the girl is a virgin.

And just as I thought, the story of the sleeping virgin upsets her balance just like on the train when she stumbled forward and fell to her knees. She insists that the child can be saved even though I have told her that the child's destiny cannot be altered at this point. She does not understand what she can change. She is irresponsible, for she really has no idea what she can do to right the imbalances but she promises me that it will turn out right.

It will turn out. That is all that is certain. It will turn. It is destiny, and it will be right because it will happen and become a new form, a new law, a new dharma.

Memsahib is horrified. She backs away from me as I tell her the story. I see her repulsion and yet my sorrow grows larger and swells so that it pushes me outward and it makes her draw back. I feel sorry for her now. She is hurt by my pain and, surely, the pain she is imagining for this child. I try to change what I am saying to her so that it is told slowly, less shocking.

"I am sorry, Memsahib. My sorrow is too great now. I tell you a story and it helps me, Memsahib. It helps me clear my karma. I am sorry. I make you unhappy like me."

This is the fact. Laxmi who is now a virgin will not be a virgin by the end of the day and she will be deflowered by a hideous sequence of men who pay to see blood. I do not apologize for this, for I am not the one who will hurt the child. I tell it straight out to Memsahib and then leave her to handle it. I am not up to doing more for her.

Georgia

What a horrible story that was! I feel like clearing a ball of phlegm from my throat, like I am being choked from within. I want to spit India out like a rotten seed from a blood orange. He has told me this news, this "information," because I insisted that I could "take it." I have become unhooked. I am unravelling. He doesn't seem to realize the effect he has on me, as if I am some unusual form of human being. Now I am the one who is out of synch as he is once again going about the business of life, trying to hail a rickshaw in front of the vegetarian restaurant. I felt that

I had regained my balance from all of the happenings last night, but I am weak again.

Karma has a childlike quality about him that drains me, much like children drain me with their endless alertness. He seems to believe I am impervious to mental anguish and, although he verbally expresses his concern for me, I feel I am the one who should be concerned for him. Or perhaps I should be concerned when he expresses *his* concern, for he has a way about him that gets under my skin. He tampers with my thin boundaries.

What an awful story! He said that the hotel where the girl is being held is close to here. On this teeming, chaotic street where the balconies, stairways, passageways, and hideaways all mix up, a twelve-year-old girl, Laxmi, is about to be raped — why call it differently? — while I, toppled by jet lag and culture shock, a foreigner, am helpless to do anything.

When I suggest calling the police, Karma lets me know vehemently that this is absolutely not the way to go, telling me that the police are in the pay of the pimps and that I cannot interfere in India to such a degree. I am close to tears from the force of his adamant rebuttal of my suggestion. While Karma chooses a rickshaw as Dahli comes hurrying from the direction of the station, I turn from them, for I am reduced to the state of a chided child. He catches my hand to help me into the shady recess and I avoid looking at him. As the driver of this battered tin transport joins the honking contest for road space, I am thankful for a rest, for I can take no more aggravating stimulus. Karma and Dahli become engaged in conversation. I close my eyes and breathe deeply.

Karma pulls my attention back to our quest.

"Today, Memsahib, we visit a place to make clean, Dhobi Ghat. Dahli brings us to Moona. Only one man more important in Mumbai and that is Dilly Willy, the Grand Whore

Master. Moona thinks you are a tourist, a famous writer from New York City. He wants to be famous, Dahli tells me, and it doesn't matter if he is famous for good or bad, just famous. Research now, Memsahib. I tell you the stories later."

Dahli disappears as we disembark from the rickshaw. Karma leads me to a break in the chain-link fence bordering the largest quantity of clothes drying lines that I have ever seen. Under the hot Indian sun, magenta, saffron, egg-yolk yellow, and paddy green saris flutter seductively beside quotidian beiges, whites, and a bunch of taupe uniforms hanging over clothes horses. Karma tells me that amongst the array of cottons and silks there are over five thousand men and women pounding to wash, hanging to dry, ironing, and folding. The rows of washing troughs and clotheslines appear to stretch to the horizon.

I catch sight of Dahli again. She comes toward us with a fine-featured Indian man. He has a slow amble, the kind of walk that will not be rushed. On Karma's advice, I pay him two hundred rupees to enter the Dhobi Ghat and he tells me that this is Moona, the father of Dahli's child.

Moona begins what seems like a rehearsed litany for tours as we walk around: "This man has paid two hundred and fifty rupees to rent a washing trough with a water tap, a drain, and a stone pounding block."

The washer draws his stature up several notches to demonstrate a hearty, well-placed slap of cloth to cement. With the fling back and whack forward, he seems to grow bigger at each upswing.

Flat irons filled with red-hot coals and lifted with deft crooked elbows by sinewy arms are passed over garments on wooden benches, cauldrons boil and bubble, soot-blackened children cluster around fires mopping food off tin plates, and everyone takes time off to glance at me; but I *study him*, this son of the Grand Whore Master. I find him cocky, with a demeanour that is misogynistic in gesture and intonation. Although Dahli had introduced us, she has not come around with us, and as if she was an embarrassment to him or he was an embarrassment to her — she slipped away.

Travelling back, Karma's mood is affable, but I am hesitant to engage, for he is strangely purposeful, as if tangentially empowered, plugged into a cryptic source. I just sit back, staring at India through the veil of the colourful fringe that rims the hooded rickshaw, and listen.

"Moona is Dilly Willy's son and also Moona is father of Dahli's baby. Another story. But first — Moona's story. Dahli has told me Moona's story.

"Moona's mother — before, many years — was new woman in the brothel. She was beautiful but bad karma, very sad, like in movies. Moona's birth — very difficult! — and he come out a little, little baby boy. The baby little but he perfect baby! Two arms, two legs, head, back, all good, but he little, little baby boy. Who is the father? Baby is born in a brothel. The mother, she sleep with Dilly Willy four nights, five nights, all week! No matter, baby too small to pass. Is better quick snap, hips, and then 'legs walk back, head front, eyes see behind, see demon wind' — old Indian words. The babies' future good now! Make money begging. Crippled beggar makes good money for beggar and Dilly Willy.

"When Dilly Willy say, 'Knees catch the wind from behind,' Moona's mother say 'NO!' She roll on top of baby, pressing baby head hard to the floor. Make his nose shut. Dilly Willy, move fast — evil fast! He push Moona's mother with foot on back of hair! He smash the mother's face on dirt floor. Moona's mother, no

more life. Die! Dilly Willy roll mother's body off the little baby
and pick up the baby. He ready to snap little body to make him
a beggar, a money-maker. He stop.

"Dilly Willy have one good karma in Dilly Willy crooked life.
Dilly Willy stop! He say, 'This is *my* son. This is Madhukant.
Moona!' Madhukant, Memsahib, it means moon, and he become
Moona — more English, more important. And the Whore Master
said 'This is my son!' and the beggars know this. Madhukant,
Moona, is power in the darkness — not light but *power*.

"Moona is son for Dilly Willy. This is good and bad karma for
Moona. Moona is big business now. He learn sex for sale, old business; old like beggars; old business, like murder. Moona is not a
guide at the Dhobi Ghat. No, Memsahib. He is the Grand Whore
Master's son. Always, he is making business in the darkness."

I am unsure what to make of this introduction to Moona and
his story but I'm beginning to understand that I must exercise
some patience with these revelations. They seem to be thrown
at me with the sole purpose of my practising my catch.

Karma

The blood-red betel juice marks India like cat spray! I must meet
one more man — more dirty than Moona. He is a crow kissing
carrion, a black rascal bird, a rat that puts his mouth over a dead
body. I will go now to the red-light district, where girls end up
dirtier than a stained cloth in the evening vats of the Dhobi Ghat.

It is like a garish circus, alive with freaks. I feel that I remember these streets and it is possible that it was very near here that
my mother might have lived in that house of many women. I
have the strange sensation that I might have been born here
or that any of these men of a certain eligible age might be my
real father, but I quit my feeble meanderings as a squat hand
branching off the shoulder of a dwarf pinches my leg and asks

if I want to buy a virgin, his stumpy fingers pinching as he tries to make a deal.

I suffer claustrophobia with each feminine glance. There are too many brushing bodies passing too close to my own, throwing out hawkish seduction from strained faces on a street lined with doorways opening onto small rooms with only a bed inside. Signs that state "AIDS" loom over this slow-minded, side-stepping crowd, and I am reminded of the dirty seed that has infected my own family. There are more horses and carriages here, only a few motor rickshaws. It is a milieu of the downtrodden. It is India's steamy sex trade, reeking.

A trade has brought me here. This and all that I have seen of this sex business is making murky the memories of my sister as sweetness; for sweetness turns sour here fast. It has cost Urban Help two thousand rupees and a promise. It is a deal, a trade that will create the karma that will move the dharma into a new position. I am here because Gurda has been paid once now and will soon be paid twice, and because he is a weak man, also compromised by his karma; I am still afraid, for I know that I am not safe coming here even if everyone has been paid off, for it is everyone-except-Dilly-Willy. From him, I must realize fear, for if he sees me....

I must trust my destiny with such firmness that I step outside of the physical, the possibility to be seen. I must disappear.

There is an alley where the smell of a stable overwhelms the street with its horsey odour. It is as Gurda has said. As I turn into it there is an intense muffling of the sound as if I am covered in the thick felt that the hill tribes make from the wool of the sheep. It is a brief moment of relief from the bombardment of horking, but the respite is lost, an untruth, and I am confined by the walls of dirty business that rise above me. It is the bowels of the flesh business. Dilly Willy's stables, a maze that smells like urine, hay, and moulding leather.

A rank sound stops me.

"Hork! Harumph! Whalork!"

A stable hand squatting on the edge of a rough hayloft above my head, his haunches drawn high, his ragged dhoti draping over the splintered beam, horks a mouthful of betel juice onto the patchy brown back of a horse and cackles at his aim. He notices me and, sucking in another snotty breath, hurls a second, and as I twist to avoid the missile of scum, he creeps away, so that when I look up again there is no one. I back into a dark alcove as I hear rustling behind me.

Someone is coming.

Gurda enters from the same direction I had come from, and with his appearance I back further into the pocket of darkness, sucked into the realm of shadows. A fleshy, pitiable sack is being dragged in under the shelter of Gurda's armpit, and as he moves into a band of dusty light, I can see Laxmi, barely conscious.

Then a distant door scrapes open, thuds shut, and footsteps come closer. A beam of purplish light from the left. There is no doubt — this is the Grand Whore Master filling a space of darkness. I have imagined that he is ugly, filthy, and awkward, a goat, garish Baliwood — all of the misshapen demons that have crowded my mind since learning of Dharma's death.

But he is elegant. White hair rises abundant above a golden complexion with not a wrinkle, although he *is* old, for his hair is so pure a white that he must be old. His eyes are like a girl's, eyes with lashes that even this dim light cannot obscure, lashes still dark so that his eyes are outlined by graceful curves. His face is held high so that he looks over his nose at Gurda. His profile defines the concept of aristocracy. There is no trace in his clothing that cuts through this image, as if he is of superior breeding, drawing formal circles of influence toward himself so that in his dove-white slippers, tastefully embroidered, nothing disturbs his beauty but who he is, the shit he stands upon, the parcel he is about to receive. As he moves forward into the dusky light of the stable, the purplish illumination from the door ajar changes to lime through the silky fine fabric of his kurta so that he seems rimmed by an eerie aura. Air moves before him, a perfumed billow.

He looks at the girl and then lifts her head up by the chin, the gesture of a man examining livestock or assessing a piece of meat. No response. He shakes her head, gripping her chin harder as if he wants her to wake up and see who he is, her Grand Whore Master. She whimpers, a bleat. He talks to Gurda with contempt, hands him a purse, and as he leaves the stables grow dark like an eclipse of the moon, an unholy darkness. Gurda arranges himself, adjusting his parcel, the little girl Laxmi. It is incomprehensible that she can even stand, much less walk, after all she must have been through, and Gurda's detachment from her human-ness is so odious as to cause me to pause.

All is silent now except the soft snorting of the horses — a comforting sound — and I know that I, too, can leave. This has been a deal, not a chance sighting, a deal with this pimp with a bad record who has to make his way to safety, where Urban Help is his only chance because his karma is strewn with traps of his own making, traps that can snap on his feet where he does not want to be caught standing. I push aside a curtain of moulding stuff and gasp the air of Mumbai with relief. I am back on the street.

It is done. I have seen Dilly Willy, the Grand Whore Master. He is burnt on my mind like a new skull blazing in the hand of Maha Kali, and I am as rank an avenger as was ever imagined. I vow to be the one who wields the knife.

The AIDS signs, stating their grim messages of doomed destinies, orient me to my direction. I decide to walk back toward the city centre, for I need to process what I have seen. The streets have grown dark to match this vision from the lower realms.

Georgia

It is my third night in India. I see that it will be essential to have some down time away from these people.

I put on a light cotton dress from the brown paper packet that the clean Muslim man dropped off by six-thirty, as he promised. I bought it at Barneys in New York, a simple beige dress, like a safari costume. I understand the origin of the scent as I press the neatly folded garment to my face. It is the Dhobi Ghat.

Tomorrow we will go to Pune, where I will meet Nur from Urban Help. Tonight, I would like a glass of wine. It seems like a slim possibility unless I go to the Taj Hotel, but since I am feeling weak and needy, I walk to the Taj, where I pay three thousand rupees for two glasses of wine and a cheese plate. Back at my room, I pop two Gravols to ensure that I sleep.

Three

Pune Prime Number One Men Only

Georgia

The air smells sensuous beneath a veneer of incense and it feels safe; there are a lot of Westerners about. I am in Pune, and Pune is overshadowed by The Humung Commune International, the ashram of Dodi Chakra, now deceased. I have heard rumours that the commune provides an opportunity for sex with multiple partners, Tantric classes, and a loosening of the strictures of monogamous liaisons. I have heard that the sultry jungle air is a conduit for moaning minions. But I am not here for this. I have come to meet Sharma's brother Nur; Sharma, and my New York friends seem so far away. Nur will be at a local brothel where Urban Help is conducting research. It has a wild name, long and pseudo-official. Karma will meet me there and bring Dahli and her little girl.

I miss my people and the easy familiarity that comes from a common cultural framework. India is confusing and I am not convinced that the experiences to date have been purposeful. Karma is from another place in all respects. He thinks differently. I'm a foreign eye observing a culture that is not mine.

I watch as a dusty naked man, a *saadhu*, walks past my sight-lines as the rickshaw slows to a stop. I see the deep ashen crevice of his muscular buttocks and I am sorry that I had not been alert and caught a glimpse of his cock. I check myself. Perhaps my curiosity is not as righteous as I make it out to be.

On a narrow hand-painted sign, in English and what I take to be Hindi, is printed PUNE PRIME, NUMBER ONE, MEN ONLY. The wooden gate is one of many in a downtrodden area outside of Pune central, with the roadside crowded with Tata trucks parked alongside metal shops and garages. I see Karma sitting cross-legged on a wooden bench and he rises as I pay the rickshaw driver, intercepting my bargaining and then handing me money that he has collected.

"Work to do here, Memsahib. Stop, one moment. You are meeting Urban Help president from Hyderabad. He working for two
months on a murder. A young girl from Goa is victim, Memsahib,
and you hear the details today. I tell you first, Memsahib, and you
understand why I work for Urban Help. The victim girl is my sister,
Dharma."

I begin to try to voice my sympathy.

"Later, Memsahib. Right now we look to the future, but my
energy come from the past. This is my karma. You will meet an
old prostitute, Ginni. She reported my sister's death. She is very
brave. My sister disappear — off the books! — when she enter
Pune Prime, Number One, Men Only. Ginni was a friend to my
sister. Jenny for English. Hindu name is Ginni. Now, you go in
the brothel — Do not mind 'men only'! — You hear my sister's
story today. Urban Help doing research right now."

Karma

I sit with the women and wait for Urban Help to tell me to come
in and listen. Dahli chatters on to me.

"I have known tourists since I was a girl in the Basilica of
Bom Jesus in Old Goa. The white-faced strangers are not so
strange to me, but this American woman, she watched me, saw
my shame and helplessness, and she, like God, is not caring about
me. Indians are strangers to the white people. They look at us like
we are on the other side of a doorway. They peer through. After
my father died, I was alone, for I was an only child. My mother
had died when she gave birth to me, so I was alone, left with
Sister Agnes — and the tourists. This is the problem with being a
Catholic in India. There are many things that do not make sense.

"Sister Agnes was white. She was a Portuguese nun, married
to the church. She left me. I was sent away, very quickly, to a
cashew factory. I had never been outside of my village, away from

the Basilica of Bom Jesus in Old Goa. Sister Agnes has no face for me now. She left me there and walked away from me. I saw her back and I remember the deep black hole that her cloth made in the path as she walked away from me. She didn't look at me when I cried for her to look at me. Now she has no face, only a back.

"I stood at a cutting machine day after day with my right leg slamming the pedal. It is not easy to make a cashew nut ready for eating, for inside the shell there is a black poisonous resin that must be removed by steaming in big pots. It escapes into the air, onto the skin, in the eyes and the ears. My job was to place the nut between the two blades with my forefinger and thumb. My foot slammed, I whipped away my hand and the blade sliced. Everything in that room was dark — the women, the walls, and the tightly closed, high windows. We were all black by the end of the day. White skin is better than black skin in India and I was becoming blacker each day. Black in my heart, black on the surface, and it was becoming harder and harder to see God. In my mind, I was not so sure, and perhaps because I doubted God, it happened. I banged down on my peddle and — WHAK! —"

As she talks, she distracts me. I am less anxious when she talks, even though these stories are awful. She is still amazed by her accident, she says as she looks closely at her deformed hand. She says that she is fascinated by the absence.

"I can still feel my thumb. It is a ghost thumb now. It's wriggling but you can't see it. Neither can I. But it's still here. I can move it from the inside. My hand, then, was horrible and I was afraid that I would die. No god was watching me. Flies stuck in my blood. They stayed and they hurt and they lived on me like I was meat. I was sick from my own smell.

"I am not a bad person, Karma. I was found. That's all. I had fallen and the spaces where I once had a finger and thumb were filled with an evil smell of sour meat. It was an Indian man who

took me in. I didn't know that he was gathering girls to be prostitutes. When I gave myself to him, it was because he was good to
me and I loved him. He was Moona.

"My life is, for this American woman, one she must pity. She
is here to help *me* up, but she stumbled and I raised her to her
feet again, only so that she could help me. I took her to Moona
so that she could identify him. It is a part of my deal. Urban Help
will help me but I must also help Urban Help."

I have been waiting here at this brothel where the walls are thick
and it is quieter than I am used to. It doesn't seem busy and I can
hear from a room the *tip tap* of a typewriter. We are in a waiting
area near the gateway and a forgotten feeling wafts over me now
and again along with a little sorrow. It is because the little girl
is here, and I remember my baby sister was little like her once.
Maria, Dahli's child, is sweet. She is dreaming her little dreams
beside me with her head on their bag.

When the door opens, I see a woman slip in, and after
adjusting to the dimness of the interior, she sits beside me. I have
only met her once, when I first came here.

Her name is Ginni and she has a very kind face, for the
shadow on her upper lip is a light moustache of thin dark hairs
and it makes her look catlike, or maybe like a hijra, the men who
dress as women and quite often are also prostitutes. Her voice is
soft and gentle, very feminine despite the masculine peppering
of facial hair.

Ginni is Hindu, her father was a Kathakali dancer. She tells us
that she has two children, now grown. She seems most intent on
Dahli and has focused right in on her as she speaks.

"I am more to know than the first fact and I expect that
there is more to you, Dahli, than the first fact, the facts that I have

been told — that you were a prostitute and are the mother of a child whose father is the son of Dilly Willy."

I like her more. She has put Dahli's prostitution in the past and is bringing her into the present through her child. I am glad of this, for the child is sweet.

Ginni continues to draw Dahli closer to her. "I am a proud mother. I, too, know how to transform, like the Kathakali. I have experienced motherhood and it is the aspect of myself — Ginni — that is my centre. You will come to know me because my karma links with your karma, but you will not know enough of me if the first fact, that you met me as a prostitute in a brothel, is all that you know. I believe, as a Hindu, that when I am present in my actions that each action leads me to another. Buddhists also believe this and we are proud that Guatama was a Hindu. This tale is a karmic tale. I want you to know who I am and I know that you will listen to what I have to say because you want to understand. Please do not feel ashamed for me or look at me with sadness and I will respect your many faces as well.

"My name is Ginni, like the precious gold coin. When I am Ginni, I can shine. But as Jenny, the prostitute, I may appear dirty, like the grimy surface of oil on the lamp shade. This oily film is hard to see through, but it is really very thin. You wash a lamp and the soot slips away from the sides and inside is the same lamp, the same bright light, the same shining gold.

"We are both the same now — you, Dahli, and I, Ginni, have the chance at a clean shade."

I like this woman. There is none of the shame here, none of the pity or the shaking of the head. She stands with a start as there is a knock on the interior door.

"Dahli, we must go in to the meeting now, only Karma and I. We will not be too long. Rest, for we will be travelling tonight."

Georgia

I finally meet Nur. He has none of Sharma's good looks and is awkward, not looking at me directly. I pass on salutations from his sister and, as if I have returned home after a journey to outer space, when we converse as I am accustomed and he speaks in an educated English like an aristocrat with a very proper accent, the hills and valleys between the East and the West flatten. In an Indian brothel of all places, I feel more at home than I have in days, in this room that could be a boardroom in a small business except for the curtains that cover the window, shuttered already against the heat. Brothel curtains. Curtains with a slightly wine-y sheen of days gone.

"I trust that you have found your guide, Karma, satisfactory?" Nur asks me.

"More than satisfactory, thank you. He's earnest and dedicated."

"Urban Help documents the stories of thousands of sex workers, 'body mapping,' and it helps us to understand the location and specific needs of this segment of the population. Karma's sister, Dharma, is a very special case. Our research is proactive on many fronts.

"Two months ago, Sergeant Manu, one of the local police, had gone to collect his 'flesh fee,' a weekly session with a prostitute which he is entitled to as a member of the Pune police force in exchange for the brothel's undisturbed continuance. When Sergeant Manu arrived here, he asked for the newest girl, Dharma, your guide Karma's sister."

I see Karma slipping in through the door with an Indian woman.

Nur has a transcript in front of him and as the story is revealed in unsettling, surrealistic fragments, he consults it periodically as he speaks. "Sergeant Manu claims to have been 'driven' — I find this word typically self-righteous, as if there was another force in control — by a 'raging need' to this newest girl, Dharma. Finding her to be bleeding — 'the monthly dirtiness that no decent man would enter' — he had forced his entry from behind. She had balked — his testimony says, and 'like a wild she-cat used her claws.' I guess they were calling her 'she-cat,' for the name kept coming up during the hearing.

"Sergeant Manu claims he was justified in beating her. And, yes, we suspect alcohol to have been involved in this incident, but at this late date we can prove nothing on that account. In some ways, if we were able to prove that he was drunk, we might have more support from the Indian public, for although Indians may tolerate a misogynistic act which falls in line with a traditional domestic hierarchy, they are intolerant of alcohol abuse.

"Sergeant Manu said the trouble began when Dharma had taken exception at his attempt to 'back-end load.' Do you know the term?"

"Yes, of course." Anal entry. I wonder how many details Karma has been told already or is this for him an excruciating telling. I am suffering for him as I listen.

"Sergeant Manu said that he 'tried the front gate with a beer bottle—'"

"How did Urban Help come in to it? What are these reports that you're reading from?"

I ask as much to stop the abrasive tale as to interrupt for information — for who cares where it came from? I am not up to this. Dharma is nothing to me and yet I weep for her. She suffered horrible abuse and now is being exposed again in this clipped delivery. I never knew her but I have begun to know Karma. I am aware that he is listening as am I and that he is aware that I am listening. None of these people are really close to me. I feel outside of them. Nur is telling us about this girl, Dharma, with such coolness but intensity that I suspect that he might purposefully be presenting graphic detail in order to raise my emotions, like a preacher recruiting for God's army against the devil. It furthers my perception that I am not one of them. I am not participating in this Indian drama, this tragedy. I am here to use them, to write a book that will be displayed in the living rooms, rec rooms, sun rooms, bathrooms, dressing rooms, any damn Western room — but not here, in this brothel where the blood happened.

"I can see that you are upset. Am I all right in going on? We held a public hearing and now are in the process of exploring legal options. Testimonies were gathered. This is the report on the hearing that I am reading from. It is just the beginning of trying to have this man brought to a full trial that could set a precedent that would radically effect prostitution in India, especially the importation of village girls into the city, supposedly to be used as domestic servants, girls who are registered as such and then literally handed back over to people like Gurda with a wink and a nudge, perhaps even an appointment made. We have managed to influence Gurda, the flesh-broker, and he is serving us in order to slow us down from pressing charges. We needed a way to draw more attention from their side. We needed a way to attract the attention of the Grand Whore Master, Dilly Willy. Gurda told Urban Help about Dahli, the mother of Moona's only child. We approached her through Gurda in order to gain her participation. It didn't take much to convince Dahli that the route we were offering out of the sex trade was to both her and her daughter's advantage. It motivated her to help us. But let me finish the story first, so that you have a bit more background."

I balk. I experience a sense of embarrassment, almost shame, as I wave him to go on. I wonder why I felt motivated to delve into this country's sex trade. My being able to dabble in the sex scene in New York — black garter belts and lacy bras, safe naughtiness — did not prepare me for *this*.

"Dharma died from the brutality she endured from this policeman who left her to die. She was just left. There was never a doctor called. Gurda was in charge. He had arrived from Mumbai, delivering a new girl, and when Dharma was found dead he became paranoid that Dilly Willy, his boss, might accuse him of the murder. He felt that he was in some kind of trouble. That was the mindset that we were able to take advantage of, for he is beholden to us now in exchange for the promise that he will not be implicated. We have a sufficiently authoritarian profile to make him afraid, and we have no qualms about using such pressure."

Nur stops. He pats his pile of papers into order and leans back in his chair, crossing his arms across his chest.

"Ginni. It's your turn now," he says without a swipe of visible feeling.

Ginni speaks nervously, softly. Again, as with Karma, I am surprised at her fluency. "I want to help you. I *will* help you, but you must understand that I am also afraid. Sergeant Manu has been coming to me for five years now. But ever since Dharma's death things have changed. When I telephoned Urban Help, Manu says I betrayed him. And I did. I felt no loyalty to him. Dharma was special."

"Now, I am the oldest prostitute in Pune Prime, Number One, Men Only. I am thirty-five years old. I go to Kochi every six months to give my family money. I have supported my two children. My mother died. My father was killed and it was in the newspaper. My children have grown up in my uncle's house. I live under good stars and my children were not closed from school."

"Did Dharma ever leave here, Ginni?" asks Nur.

"Yes, one time. Dilly Willy, he is smart. He allows the girls to go home because he knows they are ashamed. Dharma was not allowed to leave for two months. They locked her door while she had sex with ten or maybe twenty men each day. Then Dilly Willy told her to go home for a week of rest.

"Dharma went home and then Dharma came back here. She went to Goa. She told me that she was very careful to go home when Karma, her brother, was on the beach working, not in the house. She could not face the love of her brother. She gave money to her father. It is the small worth still left in this life. It is the only way she can go home — to give money. Village people do not want girls who are prostitutes to come home. The shame is two times. There is the shame of the girl who is a prostitute. There is the shame of the family. The father made the shame for Dharma. He had taken money for Dharma. He had made a trade with dangerous people, a trade he did not want to take back."

Karma is silent though his face is tense. The day is hot; the ceiling fan lazy. The air is as heavy as the weight of the crime that is resting on each of us — not guilt, but the knowledge of evil is intensely present and unbearable. Ginni is beginning to slouch into her chair and tremble slightly as if she is having a nervous reaction to her own telling.

"Dharma returned here — where else could she go?"

Nur steps in, curt. "This is perhaps the story you came here to write, but you will be a witness to a greater story if you will help us, for you are from America and we must let someone know what this struggle is, here in India. We have found a hole in the fabric, through Dharma's death and the subsequent willingness of her brother, Karma, to help us. Karma, your guide, is a big part of our plan because Dilly Willy will soon find out that the famous writer from America is being led around India by the brother of the girl who died at one of his brothels. And we have more for him, simple diversions against his effectiveness.

"Dilly Willy is not a stupid man, or even an uneducated man. He is clever and determined to maintain his power. We need your help. You have a profile just by being American and you will not disappear as easily as might an Indian. That you are a writer, this will not go unnoticed once Dilly Willy tunes in.

"It is a simple exchange. We will let you have Karma as a guide and you will be exposed to the sex trade in a manner that would be impossible for you, as a foreigner and a visible minority, to access. We will explain the path when it is necessary, but you will have to trust us. Our request is altruistic. We want to borrow your karma for two months, wrap it in with ours, and between us make a better life for people like Ginni, Dahli, and Dharma."

Altruism is a vague term to me that involves helping without having self-interest. But I *am* self-interested, and the reasons that I had for coming to India are mine, and perhaps more selfish than the motivation of these people, but they are not bad reasons, so I answer without hesitating.

"Your explanations today have helped to clarify what has been happening. I will try to exercise stoicism but I might not live up to your expectations. What are your thoughts? Do you feel I can do what you have in store for me?"

Nur looks me straight in the eye this time as he speaks. "Let's just say, bottom line, we are on a desperate edge, and if we want to maintain a tilted balance toward good, then you are a hope. I will be honest. We are overcoming a prejudice that we have against the Western world by offering our help to you in the research for this book. My sister is married to your editor. She has assured us of his goodwill. We don't like to be used for your voyeuristic pleasure or as experiments, a little less than human but fascinating and exotic. Westerners often look from a position of aloof observation. This is a long and circuitous game. For all of us, if this works, the change effected should be positive. You've met all but one of your 'team members' — Americans like the idea of being on a team, I understand — a new girl, Laxmi, will travel with Ginni, Dahli, and Dahli's daughter, Maria. You will see them periodically, for they will be on a parallel path to yours.

"You will travel with Karma and he will be your liaison with us until you arrive in Hyderabad. Bernie will be sending a photographer for your 'coffee-table book' at the end of this month — an American. I am telling you this to let you know that you are not being cut loose from Bernie and his watchfulness. You will continue to write your book and you will have material enough by the time you return to satisfy his needs.

"Is this acceptable to you? And, are you able to give over to us this amount of control? This is about the thickness of your boundaries. We have started to seep into each other, exchanging karma, busy as bees in our cross-pollination. Our East is permeated by your West as you look to the East to learn."

During his talk, my head had begun aching. I feel as if I am on a hot seat. His insistence makes me even more determined not to bound off and acknowledge that I am starting to mentally sweat. I answer that I am willing to work with Urban Help, as I said. Nur feels cool toward me and it makes me want to change his mind, to reassure him that I am capable despite the fact that I sense a prejudice in him against me as a symbol of the Western world.

We wrap up and, as I wait while Karma hails me a rickshaw and negotiates the price I am to pay, I go to the roadside kiosk and buy a coconut. I turn away from the vendor as he pounds the nail into the shell. I can't watch. My neck and up the back of my skull is throbbing.

Karma

Nur has left. He has filled me in on the travel details. Memsahib has been told. The brothel was the potent stage on which to tell Memsahib the story. She was visibly affected and left looking even older than she is.

We have been kept out of sight from the men coming in. Urban Help has paid the powers that be and Nur assures me that we are safe to remain here for the night. Little Maria is a girl who likes to make friends and I had to track her down, for she disappeared when Dahli went with Ginni to gather her things and find Laxmi. It gave me the chance to see where we are, where Dharma was when she died.

It is an old European home with some of the original furniture but there is an Indian kitchen and the beds in which the women sleep are Indian, with wooden frames and twisted coir rope. Curtains are drawn against the light as well as the heat. I understand this; there are pretty women in the darkness but old and tired women when the lights are on. I found Maria in the kitchen chatting with a dusty crone bent over her cooking, one of the very old ones who was not put out to the streets to beg when she lost her looks to age. Maria spreads cheer. I like that, but she must learn to stay close if she is to travel with Dahli and Ginni.

There is a plan that Ginni has told me.

Moona has been kind to Dahli in their parting, giving her a means to make money. It is a begging card. One side is in Hindi and one side in English:

> The bearer of this letter is a dump. Her father's name was Ali and mother's name was Nasha. She has 4 brothers and 3 sisters. All of them are dump beside this two of them have no feet hands and

are blind. After the death of father their mother
had perish herself by eagoing into well. There
is nobody to look after then any thus deserve
your help. Small donation to these helpless and
I affirm will bring you to equal to visiting all
Tirthi and Worshipping shrines Dam a man who
wil teases them suffer Govt. Certified.

RC Road, Kozhigo
Res. No 56

                                    Thank you
                                    Dr. Mohamed

A misspelled begging card. This is Moona's parting gift to
the mother of his child. There is something cheap about Moona.
There was also something cheap about Dilly Willy. Even though
he looked wealthy.

When Ginni comes to get me, it is dark and I am tired. I am
tired of most things. I have been sleeping, off and on, little times
in sleep.

She invites me, "Come, we are having a meal in the kitchen.
I am sorry you have to wait for me. You slept? This is good. We
will talk over a meal."

But this is not a home with a nice woman who is giving us
dinner. This is a brothel, and when Ginni leads Laxmi into the
dark kitchen, I can eat nothing, for a burden sticks in my throat.
Laxmi is quiet, shy beneath her bruises. She hates her life, you
can see this in her eyes. They look away, all the time. They look
away and when she speaks her words are dusted with disgust even
if she is saying something different, like "I want more tea." She
looks away at something we don't see.

Ginni tells us that today's visit from Urban Help has been a natural step to the next step. She wants to be a Buddhist nun, she says, and I wonder if that is possible, or did she go too far away from clean to ever be able to redeem herself? She says she has decided to leave here and save herself. But can she? She owes that much to Dharma, she says, and I see that these women are all messed up. Laxmi with her crazy eyes, this Ginni woman who is used up now, Dahli with her ragged begging card; it is true, "all of them are dump." Here in the kitchen with the women there is the struggle that is India and there is the struggle that is women. Maria is maybe not crazy yet. A girl. Who wants girls but the sex trade? Or men — to marry for their dowries. And to give more babies, maybe more girls but maybe boys.

All of us are decoys. The American woman will be studying us, travelling alongside, first to Karalla and then on to Urban Help. She will be taking her notes and writing her book. We are using her, as well, and she is looking at us as we look toward her. Our destinies will unfold, but still I have a dull ache in the top of my throat and I have fear at the back of my heart.

Georgia

When I get back to my bungalow, I crash. My headache is worse. The malaria medicine might be a clue to its origins, for it's been ages since I've had one this bad. But this recent revelation that I'm as much a part of their plan as they are of mine is definitely contributing to this pressure that began in the muscles of my shoulders and neck, then crept its way up to rest behind my eyes and now blooms as a full-blown migraine. Nur said that I am going to have to meet the girl, Laxmi, the one who was in Mumbai when I was. I can hardly think of it.

When I get one like this, I can imagine that a headache might annihilate me one day. I am disarmed by the numb pain. I must remain absolutely still, receptive to only the subtlest vibration, the caress of a breeze or the stir of hair upon hair or my own fingers and their soft self-pleasuring. I must preserve every bit of movement. Only essential thoughts can be entertained.

My orgasm pokes a small hole in the consuming wrap of pain and exhumes the noxious ache out of my throbbing skull. I am able to roll off the wrinkled white sheets and find the bathroom. I manage to choose the correct tap for "hot" in the shower, but it is tepid as it dribbles on my head. I stay under until the well runs dry and then smooth out the wrinkles and sleep eighteen hours straight. I awake thankful that Nur had booked me on an afternoon rather than a morning bus.

Four

The Curse of Mint Green

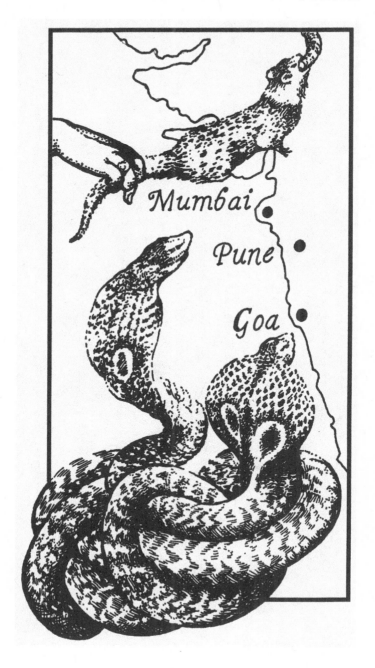

Georgia

On the road between Pune and Goa, I come to a revelation —
Indian batteries don't last. They look like American batteries
but I can only get ten songs, maximum, from my old Walkman
before it dies. Karma seems distracted, absent, when I ask for
his help.

And there is the speed issue — the bus lurches at full throttle
over speed bumps on a blind curve and then onto a bridge over
the Mandovi River, where I come undone as our driver seems
intent on being first in the neverending stream of cars ahead of
him. He passes with a series of sharp honks to warn the oncoming
Tata truck that he had better yield or there will be a joust that will
knock one of us into the river. My head, heavy from oversleeping,
jerks about more than I can handle. I feel like I'm about to vomit.

When we finally arrive in Goa, my legs are weak as I gather
my belongings. Karma will get in touch with me in two days time.
He will visit his family, he says, and neatly hops from the bus.
There is no mistaking his relief at being free of me.

Karma

Memsahib has been commenting on India since we got on the
bus. I have been wrapped in my own concerns, not so much so
as to miss what she says to me, but with a deep feeling of the
rightful position of the sangha. I can see the connections, the link
between her being here in India and my gathering my will to act.
Still, she babbles on about nothingness and I am disturbed by her
materialism.

The way to alter karma so that a new law or dharma comes
into being is through the sangha. The sangha is the community
of beings, all of the beings, from the wrathful deities who guard
against evil to the human realms to the teachers, the Bodhisattvas
and the Buddha. I deepen the knowledge of myself through

meditation and self-awareness by moving away the thoughts so that they are not a barrier between Karma, who watches, and my deeper self, the Karma who knows without thoughts. The closer my mind is to the minds of those around me, to the people of my community, the more I can make change through my karma. The sangha is made up of the people whose lives intertwine with mine. The sangha is also my family, and in that intimate grouping there was a mind that was not awake, a mind that was far below consciousness. The man who was not my father, because he was close to us, poisoned the sangha, which altered the karma and created a dharma, this path of destiny.

I am going to find him and I am going to kill him when I do.

Our journey has been plotted by Urban Help. I am to go here and there and contact this one and that one, but I am not so much following their command. I am taking Memsahib on a path of retribution. I need her as a conductor of karma. She is in a primary position in the sangha.

My father is the lowliest rung on the ladder of evil that I am climbing. I am going to Goa to kill this not-father. I am travelling with Memsahib and working for Urban Help so that they can pull me up to the next rung. They have already helped me to see who was above my not-father, for I now hold in my mind the face of Dilly Willy. There is a sangha of evil men, a brotherhood of bad intent, and I will poison their evil reptilian nest with the righteous venom of a vengeful brother.

In Goa, we will all split up for three days. Dahli says that she will have Maria baptized while she is here. Memsahib is a little rundown now and it will be good for her to roam among the tourists. Mine is a dalliance that is more purposeful, a direct connection between a daughter and a father, from one who is not a son but is her brother. Mine is a riddle of means only, for the outcome is determined. It is also a riddle of reaction, for once the courage has been summoned, I know not where this action will lead.

Georgia

Today, I am shedding the heady sex stuff and conducting a seren-dipitous meander of my own, rather unimportant and personal. I am taking a long walk along the ocean side, from beach to beach.

Anjuna Beach, where the taxi driver has let me out to explore, is at the north end of Calengute Beach. He has advised me to head south over the promontory. It was once the core of the hippie trail and there is a walking path traversing the head-land that divides the two beaches. I have no real idea how far my hike will be but he has assured me that I can make it back to my guest house via the coast and that it is not too isolated. I am moving slowly, adventuring far too late to avoid the blast of Goan heat.

I am just a short distance from the big hotels when they start to appear — dung-coloured hippies, the same shade as the beg-gar children in Mumbai. Hair is taupe. Bodies are taut or emaci-ated. The vibration is "spaced-out." I avoid eye contact, in case one of these denizens of the expatriated might think I am one of them. I leave them to their pseudo lives.

Once on the trail, I am forced to move slowly. The red Goan earth is studded with lava rocks. Prickly pear bushes and shrubs invade the path that snakes over the headland with steep ascents and treacherous downhills. As I mount a crest, I look back, con-sidering whether or not I should return to Arjuna rather than bullying my way forward against the deadening inertia this heat imposes. I see three Indian men walking some distance behind and suspect they might be the men in white shirts who had been resting at the beginning of the path. I had cast a side glance when

I passed them, striped in the shaded shelter of palm fronds. They had blurred into irrelevance. Now they feel oddly pertinent, and I flash on the strange monologue my taxi driver had initiated on the way here.

"For five thousand rupees you can have a man murdered in India," he had said. "Not a tourist, but an Indian man. A tourist is not as easy as an Indian and would cost more, but in India, all is possible."

I pick up my pace. The rocky path dips down to the seaside. I'm scared. The lay of the land contributes to my panic, twisting and turning around huge rocks, making the way indirect and maze-like.

What a silly relief as I rush around a turn and see Calengute Beach in sandy stretches ahead. I wonder where Karma might be in the reddening flesh of tourists spread before me. This is the beach where he sold his blouses.

Was I really being tracked down? Or is this my private delusion, a self-centred invention of paranoia? I think of Moona. I flash on Nur's statement that I am lending my karma in exchange for access to the sex trade. I have more in common with those hippies on Arjuna Beach than I thought. I, like them, was beginning to believe that I could trust India, that I have a place here, that I can read the signs, know a few ropes. But I am not like them. I am out of touch with my surroundings and can't even recognize where I am safe or not. I would like to know where Karma is now.

Karma

I know this place. I have stood on this very patch of sand that I am upon now, for I have walked this sand, up and down this beach, millions of times before my mother sent me away to find my sister. Three months ago I left this sandy beach, my mother, my feeble-minded brothers, and my detested father to find my little sister.

My mother had an envelope in her hand that day. An envelope with nothing in it. It was addressed to Ginni Rajpit in Pune. My mother gave me the envelope, waving her hands, hitting with her fist upon her palm, her fingers flicking me off like a pesky fly. She took back the envelope. She brought from her sari rupees and placed them in the envelope and pushed me out. All very fast. There was no father there, no Durga, none of them there that day, and I could have been frightened to leave but I know how my mother signs for "Dharma." My mother, who cannot speak, she places her hands together as if cradling a small bird and she places her invisible chick upon her heart. She was telling me to go find Dharma. And I went, and I found where she had gone, but I did not find her, for she had gone by the time I arrived.

I do not know Calengute now. I never truly knew this place, for I stayed within the periphery of my own problems, letting mischief that danced around me go unnoticed. I was not aware.

There had been wake-up calls but I didn't rise, and in the day-time I was sleepwalking. There were signs, messages from families: "Have you seen this child?" A child missing, a period of grief and then acceptance of what is to be because of what has been. Life comes and goes in India with swiftness. Life is not special like in America. It is ordinary. Indian people, the poor people, are in thin wrappings, paper cups with melting ice cream that drips onto the sand, disappearing through the grains and eventually washing out to the Indian Ocean.

I didn't engage in the selling of flesh. I never traded in lives. I was simply the blouse man. I took my share of the bodies of women, but this was an exchange, a fair deal, for I gave to them pleasure and they gave pleasure to me and it was a trade of flesh that was not tainted. They lay at my feet on the sandy beach where I walked with my blouses. They lay before me with their pearly pink, gold-and-silver-tipped fingers and toes, and when I was lucky I would follow their pretty tiptoeing back to their rooms. I have been part of a good giving and taking, lightness and easy love. My karma was right then.

Suddenly, I am confronted on my path by a vision of such evil that my stomach turns, so that bile rises and fills my mouth with a bitter taste. I see a snake of a man slithering on the sandy beach and I see this snake opening his mouth to close it around a poor and feeble creature. This is what I see: I see Gurda talking to my brother Durga! I see Gurda with his arm around the shoulder of my younger brother and I see Durga looking up at Gurda in awe and fear. I see Gurda pouring his syrupy scum into my disadvantaged brother's ear, and like a drug it pacifies him so that he transforms and begins to slither as well.

It is as clear and cold as ice — Gurda's village connection in Goa is now my simpleminded brother, Durga. It is Durga who innocently points out the troubled girls, the impoverished families, the new young widows, the love-starved girls and weak Indian fathers. And perhaps my sister, his sister, our sister. Or was it my father who first sold my sister and then looked again within his family for a new way to make money. My father, this not-father, who then brought his son to Gurda as an informant….

I can tell by the way Durga gestures, waving his arms and telling his stories. I can see by the way that he pulls upon Gurda's doti, like a dog trying to alert his master to a dead thing. I see that Gurda is indeed his master and I am disgusted enough to spew my lentils and bread onto the sand like a sacrifice to the god of revenge. And I see Gurda hand over a small rotten bag and I know that inside the bag is a bloodied payment for flesh.

And the last crowning image is to be present and watching when Gurda sucks back into the base of his nose and spits on my baby brother's retreat.

It is fortunate. It is my destiny that my eyes are so locked on Gurda's carcass that I follow him as he walks to the beach bar and, despite the distance, I hear as he taps his cracked nails on the bar-top and demands a *feni*. I see the dip in his spine as a man pulls aside the wooden beads that hang from the inner doorway, and before he is blown out by the blare of the sunlight to become an empty silhouette, I see Moona! As his white kurta becomes a blank page, an empty end to my vision, I retreat with the awareness that my family has been twice used by the man who is not my father. For who but this not-father could have introduced Durga to the underworld snakes. My not-father is a lizard among reptiles of the lowest order. I will squash him so that his kiwi green guts spill on this white sand.

Now I, Karma, am back in Goa. And so is karma back in action, ready to work and churn over a new dharma. I am back for the first time since I left home to try to find my sister. I went to Pune. I discovered the sad, filthy truth and then I sucked on every little thing that could give me life back again. I ate the facts of Dharma's death and I gained strength. I found a way into power when I met Urban Help. I stuck to them like glue and I was accepted. I had to pass many tests, the hardest being my meeting with Gurda. I kept a distance as much as I was able, for I was purposeful; I did not want to lose my opportunity for revenge. I have my own ideas of how to right the wrong that was dealt to my sister. I am full of such hate that the colours of my karmic picture have changed. I am red with hate, Muladhara, the root chakra, and I am as white as the sheet of the dead with the knowledge of my intent. When the red spills upon this white cloth it will draw a picture with a bloody ending.

Dharma did come back to Goa. I know this now. She came back with just enough energy to begin a task that I am bound to see finished. She came in through the back door, unnoticed. Strangers can find the front door to a home. It is only the family and friends who come round to the back and slip in quietly without disturbing sleep.

My not-father, scurry before my footfall like a sand crab, sideways, for I am about to smash your crusty shell! I have sniffed and sniffed, and with my breath now held I am ready to pounce.

I reach the beach hut as darkness falls. I see Mother sitting upon her bed and rocking. She rocks to the in and raspy out of her rising and falling breast. She seems smaller than I remember — thinner and darker and more sunken. Always inside herself. No way to scream. Her one eye is milky. She looks half-dead. She is a frightening mother who moves up from her shrivelled seat to embrace me, her son, the only surviving whole fruit from her distressed womb.

I tell her that Dharma is dead. I tell her that her husband, Dharma's father, had sold his daughter into prostitution. I tell her that Durga has been brought into a horrible vortex of evil and I urge her to rescue him from the influences. I choke on the words but I tell her so that she can know. My mother; my poor little mother.

Her eyes widen. She raises her hands across her face, crooking her elbows toward me. Her mouth is a gaping wrinkled hole, her complexion is pockmarked and I love her with every ounce of pity that has been retained in my soul. She is in pain like a wounded deer and I have a notion to kill her and release her to a higher life where she is whole again and young and beautiful — undefiled — and I pick up the machete, but I hold it before her for another purpose. She takes it from me and it glints with a mother's blessing as she nods her head. I nod in agreement. To kill him now is a just retribution when he is stinking from the blood on his breath, the blood of his daughter.

Mother snuffles, gesturing, and we leave the hut under the palms and walk across the sand toward the Indian Ocean and the boathouse where he has taken to sleeping. Our walk is holy. It takes time. It is a distance to the beach. Tonight the distance is poignant, like the awareness during a pilgrimage to a temple; but where we arrive there is not a sacred altar but the lair of a sloth that lives on a heap of refuse, a litter pile of boat things: rags, oily metal, grease, gas, and yellowed papers tangled in rope, nets, and chunks of disintegrating cork. There are mounds of *feni* jugs — whole, tipped, cracked, as shards or pulverized into a red dust.

He lies in his boat, the unnatural father, striped like a prisoner by the moonlight that has snuck through the boards that make up the roof. His belly is bloated and hangs in a pile off to the side like a thing other than his body, a mound of blubber like the jellyfish that wash up on the sands. His *feni* breath clouds the air so that it burns my eyes. I turn to mother to take the machete from her and stop, for she is beautiful again like the majestic figurehead of a ceremonial boat, back arched, arms held high, and the glint of the blue steel in the mauve moonlight flickers for one moment before the magnificent swoop.

Not even a whimper.

He just ends and then the waves are heard, sloshing in and out to sea, gently at peace. For a time. Until I move.

My eyes move first and my body follows as I turn a complete circle to check out what is in the boathouse. Mother wafts, drifts to the door, passes through the portal and fades from focus. I look back to see what she has done, how she has killed him, for I didn't really see. I saw only the sweep of steel, moonlit and sacred, as it plunged toward him.

His neck is slit and the blood flows, colouring the debris upon which he had been sleeping. It seeps into dirty folds, messing him, staining his soiled sorry deadness. I stare at him and see a unique-one-person unlike any other, my not-father, broken, never to be remade. Scummy life spirit — a dog, a rat, a snake, a cockroach.

It is peaceful.

I arrange his body in the boat, an offering on an altar. I pile oily rags upon him, papers, wood. I am clear as I douse the mound with lamp oil and gasoline. I envision the maleficent deity Yamantaka, who subdues demons wearing a necklace of their skulls, and I think that my not-father's head will join Yamantaka's frightening adornment. This helps me to be Buddhist in this moment so that I am awake and aware.

I make a shrine from the boat, a shrine to Yamantaka, the fiercest of the wrathful deities: Yamantaka, take this dead man's dangerous energy and transform the fear and violence that he brought with him into our lives. Help us to see with awareness and meditation.

My not-father is dead. I am free of the push and pull of his karma. The wrathful gods have gathered above and below the silence of the humble boathouse. Yamantaka is fierce in aspect but from his hands emanate jewels of clarity. From the death, there is freedom from desire. I build my shrine. I make the greasy pile of paper and debris trail outward like the spiral of a seashell so that there is a curve of cloth and junk from the dead man to the door. I light the match and concentrate.

The unnatural man who sacrificed his progeny for no good reason is licked by the hot tongues of fire as the deity Yamantaka, the terrible one, drinks the dregs of his bad blood.

I turn.

The shadows of the tall palm trees are dark, left out of the moon's magnificence. There she is, under a royal coconut palm.

She has pulled a small rocking chair away from the yard debris —
it was Dharma's — and is gently rocking back and forth in the
light of the moon. My mother, pushing herself off the sand with
her tiny brown bare feet.

Five

Warm Smells and Sharp Edges

Georgia

There is an absurdity in all that has happened and all that is predicted. I am having difficulty finding a logical path into the future. My immediate situation is indeterminate.

Karma declines my offer to upgrade his ticket, saying that he would prefer to sleep in the boxcar with the other Indians. He arrived at the train station at our planned time looking haggard beyond his years. I got a chance to put a face to Laxmi, for he joined up with the women and they all passed my window, heading down-train to the fifth class or whatever it is that they travel.

So I am alone as darkness falls, with the sound of the wheels on the tracks inspiring a melancholic hallucination of an old black and white movie, one in which an older white woman travels alone — a Memsahib — with all of the otherness that the Western world has appliquéd upon this culture being realized as a kind of racism.

Karma

I am sick with myself. I have helped to kill a man. I cannot face Memsahib with her chirpiness. I ride with Dahli, Maria, Ginni, and Laxmi, and I see that we are all broken, full of cracks. Laxmi is between two worlds, with a child's mind that has tipped into adulthood too quickly. She has become a little strange because of her being a prostitute, although perhaps it was because she was strange that she was sold in the first place. We are, each of us, a little broken, but Laxmi's cracks are the freshest and she feels the sharp edges of life more than we do.

I know now that Dahli likes to talk to me. She sits beside me and I ask her to tell me about Moona, but she tells me what I do not want to know about Moona.

"It was a close animal smell that I shared with Moona, the love of skin and the scent of hair, for there was sex and my body was free of the stiffness from walking upon this dusty India. This is the feeling that makes a family, the warm smells of skin and hair. As mothers, we know this, for our flesh has born the new flesh and it has come from our bodies, messy and warm like the monthly curse that reminds us we are female and that the blood can feed a new life when we know a man like I knew Moona.

"Now, we are three women travelling together and our smells are mixing to bring us closer. We are old and young but we are all women."

I do not want to hear about this inside story from women. Dahli visited her home as well when we were in Goa and I want to hear her babble on but not about her sex life; too much she talks about sex. I ask her about Goa now, so I can think of Dahli's Goa, not my messy Goa. My bloodied Goa.

"I find the basilica — more tourists than ever, buses parked all over in the square, and I see a priest and it might be the young priest who was there before, but I am not sure enough to signal him. He looks at me as I look back at him and I know that he has forgotten who I am so that I have no colour or form at all in his way of seeing. And I think this — I have learned how to blur, how to be invisible, as invisible as the air. It is like being a ghost, and it is as difficult to be a body and move as it is for a spirit to find a body. As I blur round a corner and down the road, the leaves rustle as I brush them and the dust shakes off my feet, but that is all that I move, for men and women never see me."

I think, *Yes, Dahli, I, too, was invisible in Goa.*

"At the basilica, I went to the graveyard where they put the bodies of Christians into the dirt and mark their places with crosses. The gate creaked open as swollen and sticky as a gluey eyelid, crust in the corners. An old Portuguese woman, black stains under her eyes, smells like alcohol, and it amazes me that she can see me when to the rest of Goa I am no longer present. I can see that she is half crazy...."

I muse, *They are all half crazy. We are all half crazy.*

"I saw her rheumy eyes looking at me as if she were studying my own face for something. I hear her whining in Portuguese and then I see that it is her. Do you know who it is yet?"

And I am diverted by Dahli's eyes for just a minute. I cannot guess who it is.

"She is bowed and her back is hunched over. Yes, yes, it was her — Sister Agnes! And I close the gate without an upward glance, knowing that she will not know me as I will never again know her except in my oldest dreams."

I wish for Dahli to distract me: *Talk on. Talk and talk to me of your little life....*

For when the blood spilled, the head of our meagre household was severed and stained the Goan earth, and as it did a purple taint seeped into the fabric of my mind. Sahasrara. The beginning of the opening of the third eye. The beginning that will change my karma.

Georgia

Karma has had a strange aura since Goa. He has told me that he does not wish to speak about his visit in Goa with such an insistence that I don't pursue it. At least he is willing to ride in the same carriage as me once again so that I have some company, but he seems to be diminishing, growing smaller in perspective.

I tell him, turning to squarely face him, that I respect him and am concerned for his welfare, and as our eyes meet I see pain and it helps me to slow down and focus on Karma. I ask him what he is thinking.

He says that because the brown skin people, like him, come from a hot climate with a perpetual growing season, they are accustomed to "many mangoes for the picking." There is not the need to plan the storage of food or the securing of shelter that the more northern peoples are tied to. Whites, if they did not organize for their winter food supply, would die, and this led to the sense of ownership in the whites that is lacking in the brown skin peoples, who see no need to hoard mangoes because they are there to be picked by anyone, and if not mangoes, then bananas or coconuts will come into season.

I had an idea of "getting something" from India, an intellectual "something," and in order to get it I formed a plan that would enable me to gain information. But now I have been asked to trust and turn my destiny over to others. I have been asked to share. Karma says that he wanted to let me know that I, too, am not alone. I believe that he is telling me that I am not as foreign as I might have been when I first arrived. I guess we're sharing mangoes.

Karma

There was blood everywhere and it was horrible to see. Even though I hated the man and wished that he would die many times, I was quiet inside when it happened, and I still am silent. I am indigo blue, for the meaning of the murder is stuck in my throat, the blue chakra, *vishuddha*. Why am I grieving? Who am I grieving for today? I was sad about Dharma but I should not be sad about a man who was not my father. Still, I have immense sadness, and only when I am engaging with Memsahib does my mind cross to a brighter soil.

I have always been eager to learn. I have read many books and I am not stupid. I was only a simple blouse man but I was also listening and forming thoughts. I was watching the thoughts come into my mind and pass out. Now I am better off sleeping, for the thoughts tumble into my mind and it has become full of phantoms, and they won't leave. I plough behind a slow ox.

I am taking Memsahib to meet a man at a perfume and incense factory. Urban Help has given me the address in Mysore City with a simple instruction. It was in my email.

The "factory" is a joke. It is embarrassing, this India. There is a woman sitting on the floor rolling incense. She is quick. She picks up a stick, sprinkles a black powder onto her black palms, and rolls the stick, out and back. She rolls stick after stick after stick — a one-person incense factory. This is India, my India, thinking big but living small.

And the perfume factory is another joke and I am sick of laughing. It is a yellow plaster cubicle with a bulky man sitting beside a table with glass, brass, and clay containers. Perfume bottles. They are cheap. No quality. On a shelf on the back wall, larger glass jars are filled with cloudy, floating things in dirty liquids. One is filled with round balls that seem to be drifting like lazy fish. I can see Memsahib is nervous as she looks at these things.

This man, whose name Nur has given me in my email this morning, is Phoolan Daichee. He has a glass wand that he dips into one of many small jars on a tray before him. He twirls his wrist and passes the wand under Memsahib's nostrils, sits back to look at her as if he can see something that we can't see, and then he wipes the wand with another foolish little flick. This is a selling trick.

After a few smells, I can see that Memsahib is beginning to relax. Her eyes wander to take in the strangeness and then her eyes stop as he keeps her in his aura. He tells her the name of the scent that cures rheumatism and another for helping sleep. He lets her have a small smell of an aphrodisiac, telling her that it is the perfume that Cleopatra used to scent the sails of her boat on the Nile, the perfume that drew Antony toward the kohl-eyed queen, and Memsahib likes the story. So do I.

"I have oils as old as your bible. I have frankincense and myrrh," he tells her, and this excites Memsahib so that she talks of the bible and her past. Then Phoolan moves his chair nearer to her and, taking one of the bottles from the table, he tips it to his forefinger. His manner changes so swiftly that I am not as quick getting up as I should have been as he grasps her left shoulder and — fast! — shoves his finger into her nose. It is rude, a penetration, and she is upset, but he is, again, quick in his way.

"I am sorry to frighten you. This is an old and powerful scent. Very long-lasting but to be long-time healing, the inner nose must drink deep. This is frankincense. It will cure your headaches."

She should be mad, for he has penetrated her, he has crossed into her body without her permission, but she is not and I do not like her. She is being stupid. "How is it that you know I suffer from headaches?" She is like a child who is pleased because she has a surprise. I am suspicious of this man who claims to heal with his oils and scents. I have heard of the men who pat their hand on the cheek and in the hand there is an oil paper that makes the victim sleep and when he awakens he is no longer a whole man, he is broken; but I continue on the path I am to walk upon despite my misgivings.

I see this is the time to let fall my message and I say it in English so that Memsahib can understand that we are not here by accident.

"You are master of magic medicine, big respect. They say you are like a medicine god, that you change karma. I talk to my friend, Moona, in Mumbai. He says hello to his father's friend, Phoolan Daichee."

Memsahib listens to me now. She buys some little bottles of perfumes — frankincense is her first choice — and we leave. She wonders how I am so smart and know these things and I tell her that it is simple: Email. I feel a little bad because I have been in on the plan and Memsahib has not.

Nur had written that Moona is on our trail. He is travelling with Gurda. Dilly Willy has every beggar who falls under his wicked spell keeping an eye open for Ginni and Laxmi. There are to be no murders. Only information will gain a purse from his cold palm. Phoolan is on our side. The visit to his apothecary was an introduction to Memsahib, for him, so that there will be no mistaken identities later.

It is important for Dilly Willy to feel safe in his chase and I am to bring Memsahib into clear sight of Moona so that he will report it to the evil suave man whom he calls father. I am not afraid for Memsahib, for there will be others from Urban Help who will meet her in Mangalore as well.

I must measure out our steps so that they fall in place with Moona's. Gurda has told Urban Help that Moona will be at the second address that was in my email, in Mangalore, on February 28. It is a jewellery store. I am to bring Memsahib to this store at the same time.

Georgia

Karma's lodgings are always included on my bill. The fee is very little. At the start of our travels together, I thought that he had a room in another part of the hotel, perhaps a division of space based on decorum because I was a Memsahib or because of a lingering sense of caste. But I learned that Karma gets a refund on the money I pay for his lodging and that he usually sleeps in the yard or hallway of the places where we stay.

Every morning I hear a knock on my door, and when I open it, there is the tray of chai sitting on the floor outside of the door. I usually rise, shower, and dress, and the next time that I open the door, Karma is there, waiting for me, and thus the mornings begin. We have a workable routine.

Karma

Today Memsahib slipped into unconsciousness and I panicked with a confused rush of feeling that I have not been able to put aside.

I was unaware of the danger. I thought the liaison was only to be a time for Moona to see Memsahib so that he knew that she was nearby and that he would continue to follow us.

I had explained to Memsahib that she might be seeing Moona. I told her to ignore him as if his presence was not unusual or as if she could not recognize one Indian from another — it was perhaps mean to say that.

She had been more relaxed and our travelling had been pleasant. When we arrived in Mangalore, we went to the address that I had been given. It was a huge jewellery store, like a palace, and very official. Memsahib was made to show her passport and to sign a paper saying that I was with her. At first, when the doorman buzzed Memsahib in, he put his arm out to stop me so that Memsahib had to insist, and then once she had shown her passport, the doorman's welcome continued to me as well, as if it was never interrupted by his gesture.

Inside it was very crowded with rich Indian women attended by young men, and many Western tourists. The big hall was noisy with the clatter of many languages.

Memsahib was given her own clerk who led her to a case sparkling with necklaces studded with emeralds and rubies. The clerk sat her on a velvet chair and helped her to try on one, then a second necklace. She had taken a mirror from the top of the case and was looking in it, frowning slightly as she turned her head from side to side with her neck held high so that when Moona entered, Memsahib did not see him. I patted the hand mirror so that she looked to my eyes and understood that it was a signal. She is not a bad actress. Her movements were slow as she glanced in the mirror and then turned casually as she placed it back down as if she was only slightly interested.

The clerk became animated, making a slight commotion over the fact that she still had the necklace on and insisting on helping her undo the clasp in the back. There were many people in the aisle. I saw nothing unusual at first, but then Memsahib leaned forward with a sucking-in of air and a widening of her eyes. Then she bowed her head and closed her eyes and began to fall. An Indian woman frowned as Memsahib brushed against her, as if she was being soiled or pushed as Memsahib's hands, trying to stop her fall, slipped along the fabric of the woman's sari.

Memsahib fell to her knees and tipped forward, bent onto her arms so that she appeared to be sheltering herself from an earthquake or a strong wind.

As if a gunman had fired shots into the room, all the people in the great hall stopped in the middle of small actions. Everything and everyone stopped, and then, in a breath, they were all alive as if the movie had come on again. Business resumed with small duties of polishing, packing, writing, and money exchanging with hushed voices as if the gems were more precious than life. The clerk had walked off abruptly and it was odd that none of the staff was moving to help me. I knelt so that I could push her onto her side and then roll her over onto her back. I didn't want her on the floor like that, with her back exposed and her face hidden like a frightened little girl. As I rolled her over, I heard "Doctor. Stand aside!" in Hindi and then in English.

The woman is a doctor from England, and between her, her husband, and myself, we managed to move Memsahib to a tourist hotel nearby where the doctor and her husband have a room. I learned that they were the people I was supposed to meet here in

Mangalore, also from Urban Help. Their presence in the jewellery store was not by mistake, but it was not to take care of Memsahib that they were brought there, but to identify Moona. Once again, "for the future."

Georgia

Before I can adjust my eyes to the low lights, a woman calls, "James! She's awake!" This startles me, and abruptly I *am* awake, feeling like I did when I was a child and I would awaken to the sounds of my mother doing things in the kitchen, for reality still seems a step away from me. I concentrate on bringing my attention up to par. I sense that I have been in danger and that I need to know *where* and *what* quickly.

I am in a hotel room. It is an Indian hotel room, decorated with Ravi Varma posters, but I don't know who this woman is. She is a short, pale woman, hardy-looking, with a practical ponytail, dove-plump chest, and a red neckerchief. She rises from a chair.

A stubby, rotund man arrives, magically, and as if on a stage, dramatically he proclaims his first line: "Well, well, how is she doing? Let's call the young man in as well."

I am glad that they speak English and I tell them this, more as a way of introducing myself than anything else, for I still feel confused.

"Speak English? Of course we speak English. We *are* English — Just call me Mandy, dear. Don't worry, you'll be fine. And this is James."

Like Alice at the height of the Mad Hatter's tea party, it is as if I am being served up as a dish, poked at with a spoon and slid around the plate. The woman announces that she is a doctor, in India for many years with her husband, an engineer. This is somewhat reassuring, for they seem quite zany.

"How long?"

"Half an hour at the most. Where has Karma disappeared to now? He was very worried for you! We are with Urban Help, dear. Not to worry. You were given a poison pat, mandranioxide, not to worry. You weren't out for long, so the dosage was small. I'm surprised they would attempt such a trick. And in a store! But of course they were all in on it. Dilly Willy has his hands in many pies and the gem business is no different."

Mandy has a Cockney accent. She babbles on. She had nursed in Calcutta. She had worked with the Mother Teresa Clinic in Pondicherry. I feel that I have relinquished something without having given anyone permission to take it, for I want to go back in her statements — to this "poison pat" — but she has changed the subject to herself and my tongue feels thick. Karma enters and I try to signal to him with my eyes that I need help, but they seem to already be in collusion, for Mandy tells Karma that the reason the perfume seller thrust the frankincense up my nose was as a protection against the mandranioxide — *this strange word!* — and I understand that they know more of my story than I do.

I am not sure who is hustling me. Although I tend to trust Mandy and her husband because they are English, their frantic conversation seems a cover-up for something else, and in comparison, Karma, with his concern for what had happened to me, seems more real. My English interlocutors are pretty quick with their exit, promising to be able to reveal more once they know, that everyone has to exercise trust, and that we are part of "something bigger than any of us could realize individually." Personally, I think this is a cop out and I tell them as much.

Mandy speaks. "Let me explain to you, dear. You were set up. We thought that Moona was being set up but somehow or other he knew ahead of time — probably the pimp, Gurda — so that when he went to his meeting at the gem store, a meeting that Gurda had told Urban Help was to definitely happen, Moona came in fully prepared to see you there. We have been too naive from our side. The jewellery store, of course, belongs to Dilly Willy's immediate boss. We knew this. He has a coffee plantation nearby and a home there where his present wife lives. But we didn't know that there would be a clerk who would place a mandranioxide patch on you — it was on your neck, by the way. Karma missed it when he turned you over. They wanted to give you a little scare apparently. Let you know that *they* know — cat and mouse kind of a game being played here — but now I know that James and I really must go. We have a car waiting. The hotel room is yours. We have booked you in and Karma has his lodgings settled as well."

And they leave with their flurrying ways, forgetting a bag so that James returns two minutes later and then dashes out again. I still feel that I am being granted crumbs when there is a big bun somewhere in the wings that they are holding back from me. I ask Karma but he says that he knows no more than I. I trust him when he tells me this.

Six

I Am a Dump

Georgia

After a rest that was not a rest in Mangalore, we are back on another train on our way to Kochi, where we will all meet up at the home of Ginni's uncle. Today we had hustled to the station early, in the dark, and I can't even stomach a banana. I don't know what or who to trust and I feel that I can't stand the suffocating air any longer. It may be the spices from the curries, but bodies smell differently here. And there are always beggars on the trains, coming in at one stop, working the train, and leaving at the next. Earlier, I had gone to stand by the open door to catch a different smell — hot metal tracks — but had stepped abruptly back as the impact of air from a train passing in the other direction on the tracks forced me inward. As I was thrown back, I stepped on a beggar. The man had shrunken deformed legs, drawn under him as if there was a shame to this dragging wreck of twisted limbs — his meal ticket. It was a horrible and frightening feeling, as if the arm itself had made the awful squeaking noise when the heel of my shoe dug into it. The man got angry at me. It was a scene, horrible and humiliating.

It is when I get back to my seat that I see them.

A little beggar girl comes down the aisle of the train, raggedy, filthy, one of a million little depleted begging beings, her hand forward, saying "*baksheesh*," and so I hand her my breakfast banana as I have no change left. Her slight squeal, for she was expecting money, rouses me from my pathetic dissatisfaction to look down at the little face. Her look of surprise broadens into a smile and there is little Maria! Behind her is Dahli, head covered, body bowed and with a snivelling gait, pulling cards from her shrouded figure as she shuffles down the aisle. I accept the card and find it hard to read, the English poor. It begins with an odd phrase — "The bearer of this card is a dump."

Thinking that I have the time to read the card, I am lazy in my attention. Absorbed in deciphering the card, I jump when the new hand touches my knee. I look up to see the girl that I had spied walking with Karma and the others that morning as we left Goa — Laxmi. Her face flickers on for a minute, like a surge of electricity, but then she shakes her head like she wants to move her brain into action and a charge leaps between us so that I flicker on and look more closely. She has changed from the young woman I had seen in the brief sighting I had of her from behind the train window. Her eyes are yellowish and puffy with dark circles below them. She looks at me — watching the other passengers, as well, as if she is expecting an explanation from them — and then back at the coins in her palm, and she rattles them once more. She looks like she is trying to remember why she wants the rupee. She has an aura of being overwhelmed and yet barely present.

Laxmi horks — without meaning to, an involuntary hurtling of phlegm — onto the rupees in her hand, and her smeary eyes rise to lock with mine when we both see the blood. Horking is a constant part of Indian life. A "hork" collects in the gullet to become an exaggerated clearing of the throat, an expulsion of the guck that has filtered past the discerning hairs of the nostrils or passed through the mouth when it opens to eat and drink. It's a background sound to India as consistent and ever-present as the honking, a necessary expulsion of the inequity between a person's intake of India and what can be digested. There is just too much to be processed in India. What's left over comes out. Yet this hork does not signal pollution to me, but sickness. Her hand is covered in blood.

Then she is gone just as Maria has disappeared and Dahli, in a rush of beggar movements, and I understand. I have received this message, clearly. Laxmi is not well. The women have been travelling alongside of me since we left Goa but we have had no communication. They have come begging down the aisle of my train car to tell me that something is wrong with Laxmi, and since we will be meeting at the next stop, tomorrow, my knowing of her sickness can't wait.

Karma

I see my stepfather more now that he is dead, more than I did when he was alive. He pulses in my head with a putrid green pulse — Anahata, the heart chakra, the green chakra, is hurting and flooding my being. He was a bulky man with a thick neck. He moved like a plodding steamer. He lay like a beached whale. He rose into the night of his low decisions, his head bent low. His stride was little, short steps with his thighs brushing. He looked neither left nor right but always his eyes were pointed down, below all hearts, downward to the floor of his possibilities. His measure of worth was small.

We travel. Memsahib is kind and she helps me to not hurt as much, and she does not even know my pain. Turning away from the troubles in my head and living in the present, I am again Buddhist. When the dark green flush of fatherly hate overtakes me, I move outside and find Memsahib, and she is always happy to see me and, always, she needs something. I keep a close eye on her, for she is younger than her years, young in her understanding of the world. Her concerns are simpleminded, not because she is stupid — she is not stupid, but very smart, I can see this — but she lacks the depth of pain. Her suffering is like skin, on the surface, not below in the guts where pain likes to live, in the darkness of our bodies. When I hurt, I leave my darkness, pull myself up, and I help her. I help her find an orange in the morning and bring her chai. I help her understand the words that she hears around her and to bring her to the India she wants to see. And as I help her with these stupid little details, she clears away the big demon inside my head with her immediate needs.

I keep an eye on Memsahib. I keep the other on Laxmi, and when I walk to the back of the train and they are not there, I panic, but when they come back and tell me that they have seen Memsahib and that she has seen Laxmi, I panic even more. I am afraid that Memsahib will be upset because Laxmi is sick.

Illness creeps and crawls on all fours. It enters the room below the vision and we miss it coming in. It is not until it stands up, rears up on its hind legs and sways from the unaccustomed height that we are able to see it. Illness is not a strange beast. It is a blood beast like we are. It is a part of us, but illness is not welcome and the shunning turns illness to cold and so it is not a part of us but *apart*, because it is cold and we are warm. Illness is a cold-blooded thing. It makes us frightened. We shake and shiver in its presence and then it moves. It strikes. Like a cobra, it sways and then it strikes. Illness is a snake.

I fear for Laxmi now. I fear that the snake has taken over Laxmi's body. She shivers, she shakes, she cries in her sleep, and I fear that her blood is losing warmth. And now Memsahib has seen Laxmi, too, and Memsahib, she does not understand pain.

But Ginni lets me know. She takes me away from the women.

"It became more than we could handle, Karma. We had to show the white woman our Laxmi. The inside will not stay in. She vomits her food, she shits out blood and black squid ink. It is not the food that makes her sick. It is something inside her that is growing bigger. It is hard, a dead lump in her belly that is in the land of death already, trying to suck Laxmi in. It takes away her warmth so that she shivers. It gnaws at her belly so that she cries in the night. She is frightened. We are all frightened now. We thought we had gotten away, but we were tracked down by death."

Laxmi is changing colour. A yellowish colour, like the custard fruit, pale yellow and greyish. Yellow is the solar plexus chakra, Manipura. Once she blended with our healthy brown skins and then she began to separate. The food comes up from her belly but her belly is big while her legs and arms are going smaller. Rapid slither of the cold snake.

I am afraid that we will make for Memsahib some kind of crazy danger. Memsahib saw Laxmi. She is not blind. She saw that she was with Dahli, Ginni, and the little girl. She would know it was Laxmi. The eyes, she must have seen the eyes. Laxmi only sees her own eyes when she looks in a mirror and she doesn't look in mirrors. She says she is ugly now and that she knows who she is without looking for herself in a mirror. We are the ones who must look at her. Anyway, we are the ones who tell her who she is. All the time. We tell her she is good. She needs lots of telling.

Fast. The snake moves fast, like life can move too fast for us to see what is happening. The snake moves fast and blurs so that we are not sure we have seen it. But we are sure now.

Maybe Laxmi is going to have a baby. Her stomach is big, she is sick when she eats. She is yellow. What baby is making her yellow? What snake found its way inside her to turn her yellow?

Georgia

At the Kochi station, we fly from the train in a rush. I had asked Karma if he knew that Laxmi looked horrible, that I had seen her, but he has been avoiding me with a direct stubborn refusal to talk about it, insinuating that I am making a lot out of nothing. I don't need to hear this from him and we argue about my ability to deal with India, for it is being said over and over within me, the same thing, that I am at odds here. I feel stupid despite my degrees and supposed Western advantages.

Karma rushes me onward from my concern, for we must find
the address he has been given and there seems to be trouble with
the driver. I feel nauseated, for it is morning before breakfast in a
fast, stinky rickshaw in another town filled with exhaust fumes.
The hustle and honk is stupendous. There is a creosote smell
coming from the braziers cooking chicken dumplings that are
set under tented coverings. Muslim fare. The markets are brisk
with masculine commerce. I drift away from thoughts of Laxmi
as my own body's discomfort overtakes my concern for her. As
I breathe deeply to quell my nausea and step out of the tinselly
rickshaw — finally — at the address that Karma has gotten from
Urban Help, I see *him*.

Sitting on the stone wall of a small fountain under a single
banana palm, a very white man reads. He looks up with a slightly
furrowed brow, but he relaxes his shoulders when he sees us, as if
the ground has finally accepted him being here. He has on shorts,
hiking boots, and an orange cotton golf shirt that is sticking to his
skin in a pool of sweat so that on his chest there is a soaked borsch-
coloured pattern like a heraldic crest or an ink blot. As he smiles,
I move forward. He appears kind and I have an unreasonable urge
to throw myself into his arms.

He stands as I come forward — a formal gesture. "Hello,
Georgia. I'm Nelson. Bernie has sent me a little earlier than was
planned." A no-nonsense, cool voice.

I balk mentally and blurt out, "I'm not sure I'm ready for
you. I wasn't expecting to see you before Hyderabad," and regret
the curtness before it has even reached his ears.

"Bernie is a little worried about you, I think, and I'd asked him
to move on a little quicker with sending me back out in the field.
Could be that my request fulfilled a karmic niche in his mind."

My inhospitable front melts from his affability and I am able
to be nice to him, for he is back in proportion, not as white and

intrusive as I had first perceived. It is like the transition back to
my own country after a period of foreign travel. I had been away,
now I am back. As my attention turns to him, Karma hustles us
into a courtyard and past a sign in English for a theatre, and I
relax a little more as if this is common, to be ushered past the
familiarity of Roman numerals, with a white man called Nelson
(what an English name!) who tells me that he has brought me a
bottle of wine. I resent the interjection of Karma's pointed urg-
ings to move into the theatre, for I would like to know better
who Nelson is.

"No time to talk now, Memsahib. First thing, Mr. Nelson
meets Mr. Rajpit and you, too, meet Mr. Naruba Rajpit. Things
moving fast now, Memsahib. Time to listen. Time to listen."

I didn't realize how lonely I was, that I would tremble, become
disoriented, insecure, and nervous just because I am walking in
front of a man who looks like me, has skin with freckles, laces in
his boots, a bank account somewhere. I am delighted with him
talking, whatever he says, for he uses words that are subtle and
yet beautifully complicated. He speaks of small and silly things so
that I forget for a minute the big hard questions that are India. He
is polite. And I, too, begin to speak of small silly things without
feeling that I might be offensive or not adequately serious in the
face of the big, sad, sour subjects like prostitution, where there
is so much pain. It has gotten to me, this juggling of mysterious
balls of fire, the handling of substances that sting, for they are
unknown to my Western, white, waspish, womanly, and spoiled
way. When he says that he has brought me a bottle of wine, I
ache in the root of my lowest chakra at the thought of drinking
it with him and talking more and more of things familiar.

But there isn't time now and, as always, I am hot again, hot
from the simple exertion of arriving in the little theatre that is a
space the size and shape of an American garage, with a ceiling

made from rows of mosquito net seamed together and then stretched to cover what appears to be a brick roof with open sky-lights. Mosquito coils burn under the chairs although there is no audience; the theatre is empty. A string of Christmas lights defines a stage, and on it sits an older man with the refined features of a figure in an Etruscan fresco — high cheekbones, big limpid eyes, and full, distinct lips. He appears to graze on our expressions as we are introduced. He is Naruba Rajpit, Ginni's uncle.

"Welcome to my little theatre in my private, very private, courtyard. My theatre presents Kathakali — a religious ceremony as well as a dance performance. At one time it would have been done only in a temple and all present would be cleansed as they watched the familiar tale being enacted. I perform in English now because Kathakali interests the tourists.

"I have performed this show every day since I was fifteen. I began with my father. We built this theatre. A dirt floor. The Indian people are strongest in one thing. We need only a dirt floor. We could have a cement floor, but in the temples, this dance is done on a dirt floor. Here the floor is dirt, too. We don't need the cement. This is where the Indian is strong. He knows what he doesn't need.

"And *this* is not needed — two nights ago, a slimy pig eager to climb up the slippery ladder of evil gave me this address, on this piece of paper — 'Shamballa and Rajiv, 53 Samptan Road, # 571, Delhi.'"

Naruba's forehead creases as he explains that this is the address for Ginni's children and that he had been told by the "slime-pig" that they would soon die, a simple method, a simple brush to the skin with mandranioxide.

I see that Nelson is listening intently. His face has turned the same beet colour as the sweat on his orange shirt. He is engaged beyond my power to distract him.

Naruba Rajpit talks slowly and clearly. "Mandranioxide is a poison. A horrible, numbing drug. You see, this poison would make my niece and nephew feel faint, and when they awoke, out on a street, *if* they awoke, they would be missing a kidney, a liver, or maybe worse."

Naruba's story, despite his careful delivery, flares with the hot pink light of danger, but it is Nelson who appears to be flashing a red pulse.

"The slime-pig said that they will scoop out my pretty girl's heart," which is when Naruba's face disassembles and his elegant features collapse in a mixture of fear and grief.

He tells us that he had felt guilty. He says that the man who killed Ginni's father, many years ago, is Ramone Sanchez. When, recently, an organization called Urban Help had gotten in touch with him, he had complied with their plans and had asked Ginni to come to him, to be here when Sanchez was released, for Urban Help had promised him that in exchange they would help Ginni to leave the sex trade forever.

"I can create my karma but I must also go along with my destiny. I did not know if Ginni would come home. She must come, I told her, but I left this to Ginni, to determine if this was her destiny. But karma is linked and I did not think that I was placing Ginni's children in danger."

As I watch Naruba's brown, damp face, I see his sorrow, and I look over again at Nelson and see that his face is also creased with worry. Suffering connects the fibrous paths of humanity. Each man, immersed, has lost sight of a middle way that evens out extremes. I have not an inkling of what it is that is fuelling Nelson's anxiety, but it seems to be in synch with Naruba's.

I feel slightly intimidated by my sense of prescience.

Naruba looks at me squarely as he speaks. "This young man who calls himself Moona, in his Western clothes, with his sunglasses and lazy airs, he said that he knows that the white woman — you — is also watching the runaway women, and he said that you are writing a book. He is interested in you. I am hoping that you will lead him away when you leave here — you who write a book on our women in their shame with our Indian men.

Naruba turns his attention to Nelson to say, "Rajiv and Shamballa, how to protect them? I have on a fierce mask but I have fear on the face behind the mask, as well...."

The heat makes thinking an overexertion. I am humiliated by Naruba's assertion of my low esteem, it having been said in front of this man who has just met me, Nelson. We are all now so wrapped up with problems that time drags, and an eyebrow raised, a forehead furrowed, a mouth pinched registers in an exaggerated mode. I feel like there is a cloud of flies above my head. That I am unclean. That I am a cause rather than a possible solution, and then, thankfully, Nelson responds.

"I can help you here. I know a man in Delhi. A very good man. Hamid Balik. I have worked with him before. He has international security status. I'll email him. Give him the address for Rajiv and Shamballa. Ask him to hide them. He has a large family."

It's beginning to cool in the small theatre and Naruba calls for chai. Naruba questions Nelson and is satisfied with the arrangements. I relax after Nelson's having been able to take control and I tell Naruba what I know about Moona, his wife Dahli, and their child, Maria. When I say that Dahli seems to offer his niece some protection, for surely even Moona wouldn't hurt his own kin, Mr. Rajpit looks at me as if I, too, am now human rather than just trouble.

"I will tell you something. Kathakali see things other people cannot see. I saw something in this Moona's eyes. I saw lost goodness. We are all linked by *karma*. It is like the lights here in my theatre — one dead bulb on a string of lights and that one bad bulb turns the others out. Put in a good one and boom! It is all light!

"Now I tell you why Urban Help takes time to know us. Ginni's father fell in love a second time, many years after Ginni's mother died, with a woman, very beautiful, but married to an evil man. Mr. Daku Man Singh. He is a judge, big man in Mumbai. He is a crooked politician. She was a Bharata Natyam dancer. She and my brother danced together.

"My brother and his lover were discovered right here, in this theatre. They spoke only once after that when she told my brother this name, Dilly Willy, in response to his question as to where she was going, for her husband had told her that she was being sent away. Then Shauna Daichee Daku Man Singh — this was her name — disappeared.

"My brother looked everywhere for his dancer. Then he met with Sanchez, I think hoping to find Shauna. I do not know why he trusted to meet with this man but they met in the Windsor Hotel above the harbour, Fort Cochin, in Kochi. A bottle was broken, my brother bled to death, and Sanchez was arrested almost immediately.

"Daku Man Singh — he makes the shadow puppets dance. Sanchez, he stayed in jail. Nobody saw the beautiful dancer, Shauna Daku Man Singh, again.

"Dilly Willy — it's not a name that one forgets."

Karma

There is a thread itching me, hanging below the reality fabric. If I could see where it connects into the fabric, I could tie it up so that everything doesn't unravel, but I can't make sense of where it is; I can only feel it rubbing against my skin, and it is more an irritant than a tickle. All worlds lead back to Dilly Willy. When there is an

evil deed, it goes back to Dilly Willy. If the lover of Ginni's father
went to Dilly Willy, what does that mean to me? When I hear this
name, I think where it connects into the fabric. And I know from
the name of this other man, Mr. Daku Man Singh, the husband,
that he must be a descendant of the famous Daku Man Singh, the
most famous dacoit of the Thuggee sect. You can tell much from
our Indian names. There is more to know, more that is just below
the surface.

Memsahib is with Nelson. This is good for her to have a man to
help her. He is a smart man, calm and in control of himself so that he
can also help others. Memsahib needs someone to settle her down.
I am glad she didn't see Laxmi tonight. They arrived as the rickshaw
pulled away but Memsahib wasn't looking anywhere but at him.

In the safety of this courtyard, decorated with lights that hang
from the trees, we try to work magic. Each of us. Poor Dahli is
trying to sort things out and having some difficulty. She whispers
to me as we stand beside Laxmi's bed. "All I can do is pray, it is
all that I know — asking for help from God, but my prayers must
be too weak to be heard. They are like my hand with two fingers
missing. God, the priests said, is like a right hand — useful. But
not for me, with my weak prayers unable to flutter up to His
ears. I think that He no longer listens to me. Maybe He never
has listened to me, but I don't want to take the chance and not
try to send up a prayer. Laxmi has been hurting for days and God
has not helped much. Laxmi — I think she has the sickness that
comes with prostitution."

We freeze in the courtyard, cold and still, as if the snake
might crawl from Laxmi and choose one of us as his next victim.

Ginni, Laxmi, Dahli, and Maria, all now are right here, and
Moona, like a rat smelling cheese, is nearby. He is insolent. I saw
him, I am sure, but he took off when Memsahib and Nelson left
to find a hotel.

Georgia

There is a tent in back of the hotel, prettily peaked, mirrored and tasselled like the curtained boudoir of a nomadic aristocrat. As the day loosens its hot grip to its cooler, calmer opponent, evening, and before the heavy blow of night knocks out the feisty dominant light, we enjoy the bottle of wine, and then a second, nestled in a surround of pillows. It is an exotic backdrop, a little awkward and too romantic for a couple of seasoned journalists whose only bond is a book contract, but it transcends the immediate with a wave of insouciance. Inside the gauzy, filmic enclosure, I rapidly tell my story to Nelson, almost embarrassed by my own over-eagerness. He seems so normal, as if he alone is gathered together in a world that has begun to fray, and I spill my tale with a gush of relief — about watching Dahli, the deflowering of Laxmi, and an overall impression of how horrible this sex trade in India is. I meter out the exposure, for I desperately need an ally.

"We have a lot to tell each other, Georgia, but if you don't mind, I am jet-lagged, bus-bruised, and now somewhat drunk. It's a lot to take in. We must learn to trust each other first. I am here for personal reasons as well as the obvious.

"My life's a bit of a mess. I have just left my wife and, in her care, my beautiful little five-year-old girl. For years I had been accepting war assignments to escape the war in my own home. But that wasn't what threw me. There was a full stop in my life when I lost my twin brother last year to AIDS."

Rapt and yet self-conscious, I am ready to listen, but he stops and looks at me. He smiles. He looks tired, and I, too, smile when he says "motor mouth and exhaustion…."

Nelson gathers his things, and with his shoes in his hands walks toward the hotel. I watch as his back blurs, then turns black in shadow as he disappears into the dark lobby.

Seven

Pulsations from the Crystal Ball

Georgia

I manage to drag myself out of bed in preparation for leaving in time for our eight o'clock rendezvous. Having grown unaccustomed to wine since being in India, I believe I drank more than my fair share last night. But then, to spite the early start, Karma comes back from the station with word that there is a strike on and that we will have a better chance tomorrow to get out of here. He suggests I find a way to amuse myself for the day — *a little condescending?* — but first I let him know that I must go to Naruba's, for Karma has told me that the women have arrived and I want to check on Laxmi. I ask him to call us all a rickshaw while I find Nelson.

Nelson sips a coffee in the tent behind the hotel. It is not so clean now that I see it by daylight, nor as romantic, and Nelson isn't quite so handsome. He looks like he is in the grips of jet lag, with puffy rings round his eyes as if he's allergic to the morning and is having a reaction. He has a BlackBerry and manages to send off an email to his friend Hamid asking him to help us. His friend agrees to pick up the students and take them into hiding.

With a new militaristic agenda, Karma seems to feel responsible for moving the troops on, so we do as we're told and bundle into a lone rickshaw. The streets are hauntingly free of traffic. Sitting beside the driver, Karma turns and talks pointedly with Nelson rather than me. I seem to have tumbled down in the hierarchy, with Karma and Nelson sharing a common ground of masculine efficiency. It's fine. I'm tired and blank. I have nowhere to go and nothing is being furthered, which is not only abnormal for me but this shapeless lack of destination seems to have overtaken Indian life in general. Usually abuzz with people, there is no one on the streets. Karma tells Nelson that it can be dangerous to be out during a strike. It signals support of some kind for the opposing side. I wonder how he managed the rickshaw.

There is no theatre today, and while Nelson pays the driver I go to check on Laxmi. An odour like steamy wet wool signals sickness in a corner of the courtyard made private behind a folding bamboo screen. Dahli and Ginni have managed to organize somewhat and there is a seeming safety in the ritualistic handling of the cloth as they draw it under her chin. Laxmi is shivering. She rouses, foggily. She talks with a look of confusion as if she is on a bad trip and in the dislocation of sickness; I feel that I understand her, this girl that I have only heard tell of in her most helpless hour, not knowing what she is saying precisely but having a sense of the chaos in her head.

Ginni touches my hand and breaks the cats cradle between Laxmi and me with her gentle voice. "She begins to talk but cannot finish. Her words come out in the wrong places. She tells you that she wonders why." There is a wondrous lost look on Laxmi's childlike face as she looks up at me. Ginni continues. "She says, 'nine … and the little lizard…?' I don't know, Memsahib. She is not right in her head. I don't know. She wants to tell you but she cannot."

Nelson is at the far side of the open space where birds are chirping, oblivious to any ambient distress. Knowing that he is close and that I am not alone, I can make decisions easily. I interrupt the passive rhythms, command attention, and become responsible in that abrupt Western way, swinging into gear, issuing orders and doubtlessly appearing a little mean.

When Nelson sees Laxmi, he takes over, and what needs to happen comes about with very little stress. With Nelson's cool support we arrange the transportation of the disoriented and feverish Laxmi to a hospital emergency room.

Karma

I have seen how hard it has been for the women, more and more difficult begging with Laxmi, too weak for anything, like an old person nearing the end; she can't even walk, with ankles swollen and lumps under her arms, so that even when she is still, they stick out from her body at an odd angle. And Laxmi smells bad, like a big dead mouse.

I was afraid Memsahib would be angry with us and say that it is our fault. But when you see someone so ill, it is not possible, I think, to blame. It is destiny, and Memsahib, she saw Laxmi on the train. Destiny had to unfold without Memsahib pushing too hard, so I took her away from Laxmi. Now she moves. If Memsahib wants to move fast now to help, I think so, too. Nelson told us that it was necessary. Nelson brought Laxmi to the hospital.

Ginni picks up the mess that has fallen around the bedside and folds things. Dahli sticks close to me and I let her talk.

"My Maria is a brave little girl, or maybe it is not brave, but just the way that she is. I have not been a good mother. Naruba is more like a good mother than I. See, she plays with Naruba now, with his puppets. He sees the needs of people in his care and he gives them things before they have to ask for them. In Mumbai, I didn't look at my Maria and think *What would she like to have? What would she like to do?* I thought instead *What can I do with her, where can I put her, who can I get to look after her?* All the time, two lives to look after — nails to cut, hair to wash and comb, clothes, food, and safety. I was afraid that some man would get at her. It is hard to trust women who need money and it was women who I had to ask to look after her. We did this for each other, watched over the children, but we watched each other as well, for we knew that we were only women.

"I want Maria to be safe from this danger. Ginni and I will be travelling close to Memsahib and the man who has joined her and they will help us to get to Urban Help in Hyderabad where there is a school for the children and Maria will be safe. Moona is following. He knows that we have come here. Naruba has told us this. If we travel with Memsahib and Mr. Nelson, how will they know what we need if something goes wrong and they don't speak Hindi? I am still afraid. I do not want to be near Moona when he gets mad."

Whatever she says, I tell her she is being a good mother. I praise her bravery. I assure her that she will be safe in Memsahib's care, especially as there is a man with her now. I remind her that Ginni speaks English, there is no problem. It is important to tell the women, for men to let the women know that they are strong. They see us, men, as strong, but they are stronger than men when they protect their children. I see that it is different for women. I remember my mother. I think of my mother. I remember my mother when I was a little boy and she was beautiful. But I think of my mother when she was strong because she did not have any other way to correct karma than to kill her husband. And she did it.

Things are settled quickly when Memsahib and Mr. Nelson come back from the hospital. We will all sleep in Kochi for one night more. We have come here to know Naruba's story, but this is only a small aside in comparison to the main. We have come here because Urban Help has told me that they have been following this case for many years, precisely with intent to move when this happened. Ramone Sanchez is to come out of jail tomorrow. Urban Help has arranged for me to meet with him, and we will talk. It is the time for men to be men.

Georgia

The relief of being able to turn over some of the arrangements to Nelson, who ups our ante to the added comfort of a first-class carriage, makes for a pleasant stretch.

Ginni, Dahli, and little Maria are in the bunks opposite and I have been enjoying their company although I have no real sense of them without being able to speak Hindi. They seem excited about the travelling conditions and I am glad to be able to give them this small comfort. We are to get off in Pondicherry to see Mandy and James in Auroville, a Bernie arrangement through Nelson. Ginni, Dahli, and Maria will continue straight on to Hyderabad and safety. Members of Urban Help will meet them at the train station.

I place my note pad on my lap and try to sort out some of my impressions. It's been one month since I arrived in India. Karma will meet us in Hyderabad. I miss him somewhat. He has integrity and, despite the cultural differences, we meet on a relatively honest plane.

I have no idea what is in store once we arrive in Hyderabad at Urban Help. Laxmi is in the care of the Indian health system and Naruba will care for her once she recovers. Nelson made arrangements. There was a lot that had gone wrong with poor Laxmi, all connected to the thyroid and also hepatitis, with infections compounded by her being HIV positive. We managed to get some more advanced drugs through Nelson's contacts but the cocktails that the American HIV-positives rely on are hard to access here. I am pledging that this will be my personal follow-up.

During our long wait at the hospital, Nelson revealed the source of his stress. His twin was the subject of that story that Bernie had told me before I left for India. Nelson and Norman. Norman was in India, and it happened — the drug on his cheek with the stolen organ discovered too late to arrest an aggressive decline into full-blown AIDS. Pneumonia claimed his life.

Karma

There is nothing said for many minutes. Ramone Sanchez is a foreigner despite the years he has spent in an Indian jail, even if he speaks my language and smokes a *bidi*. He is a stranger to me in every respect. He looks at me so hard that I feel precarious and disturbed. We drink Coca-Cola in a bar and there is a ruffle of dissatisfaction at this — not from me, not from him, but from the men around who think they are men when they drink alcohol together but who know nothing of the things that men do who murder. This man knows, and it is because he knows that I will know him.

Ramone lays it out first. "You are a man who wants something from me. What is this Urban Help? I have agreed to this meeting because I, too, want something. I am telling you this because I have had a long time to think and I know that I have figured it out. I know who I am. I have just spent eighteen years in a filthy Indian jail because I killed a man. I killed a man for five thousand rupees and my freedom. I have known the world as a hole. A smelly hole."

Ramone is murky like a pool where it is hard to see a reflection because there is no light around. When he speaks, his words leave unfinished thoughts so that I must guess what it is that I am responding to. He begins a sentence and then it ends slightly away from where it began. Then his head drops back and he stares at the ceiling fan, sighs, or tries to find more air as he closes his eyes for a minute and breathes in deeply.

"I left Spain for India and whores, drunk, and because I have fast fists and had to flee. I was a goonda for Mr. Daku Man Singh. I goonda for Mr. Daku Man Singh, for the great one, the politician, Mr. Daku Man Singh, an old man whose wife had a lover, so he told me, simple instructions: 'Make him shut his mouth, the lover, the fool, silence him forever.'"

He pauses too long and I am about to speak when he does. "Mr. Daku Man Singh sold his wife to Dilly Willy, his friend, his business partner. I have never seen Dilly Willy. Few have. He is the Grand Beggar Master of Mumbai and he controls prostitution. Mr. Daku Man Singh put his wife into the sex trade in

Mumbai, to punish her. And her lover? Duma Rajpit, this lover, thought I was going to tell him where she was. He offered me five hundred rupees but Mr. Daku Man Singh, my boss, he gave me five thousand to silence this man. Easy choice. I thought.

"But I was arrested, for when I met with Duma Rajpit, he said he would kill me if I didn't tell him where to find his lover — an athletic-looking, strong, wiry man — and he moved fast as a mongoose. He took a bottle to me so I cut him down. In a bar. Was caught. Went to jail and never came out. Until now. I am out.

"Mr. Daku Man Singh betrayed me. Five thousand and my freedom! That was the deal. You don't betray a goonda. You don't leave a goonda in prison. The man I was set up to kill, this Barata Natyam dancer, was a loved and respected man. These Hindus like their dancers, like movie stars. So I stayed in prison.

"Mr. Daku Man Singh. I was in prison and prison was a damp dark hole, foul, full of humans from holes and humans who are nothing but holes...."

He spits into the air.

"Crows caw ... graze on guts ... vultures know ... ass ends from ears ..."

He stops. His head rolls back and he breathes long enough for me to say "Urban Help will pay you even more to help lead us to Mr. Daku Man Singh. He is protected by many goondas, all organized now by this man Dilly Willy. Could you —"

Bolting upright, Ramone Sanchez answers. "Could I help bring down Mr. Daku Man Singh? Little man, Urban Help, whatever you call yourself — you are offering to pay me to do what I want most in the world to do."

We Indians have separated our bodies into hemispheres for the clean and the dirty as a way of staying healthy. We eat with our right hand and clean with our left, but our Indian way never quite works, for we have too many tasks that must be performed with both hands. When I cut with my right hand, what holds the food still so that when the knife falls it hits the mark? Revenge. There are many bugs in the Indian's stomach, for we eat and drink in the company of flies. Even the great white man, the foreigner, becomes loose in the bowels, for the hands become dirty as we pass filth back and forth.

Georgia

He kissed me last night just before we went to our separate rooms — a beginning, a passing moment, or the talk of his brother bringing an awareness of death and the way that awareness brings life's shortness to the fore.

If I were to become involved with Nelson, would it sharpen my take on India, I wonder, and, for that matter, do I want "my take" any sharper? I've been pricked with enough force already and this respite from the pokes and prods of Mother India is welcomed. I usually feel more alive and engaged with the dynamic of a lover but this is not just about me — and Nelson is on a grief mission. He may not have any loving reserves. Still, he is a strong personality. Everyone responds to him positively. The Indians even admire his physicality. He falls in line with a perfect soccer body, apparently, and India is wild about soccer. He does have a nice solidity to his build.

And does he want me? Do I even have a choice in this matter?

We talk a lot but we neglect to mention the "coffee-table book." I couldn't care less right now. It seems like a cruel project, wrongly motivated, eking out fame and fortune from the pathos of others. The sex trade in India, what I have seen of it, is a sorry space peopled with broken women and a few broken men. The ones around me are hoping against unreasonable odds, to my mind, that they have a potential for a productive future. All of us racing toward Hyderabad. For what? I want to just lay my head on the chest of this Irishman, Nelson Finnegan. I like him a lot.

Karma

There are two streams of karma. The mainstream is the family. More like a river fed through many generations, it is the rush of water that bursts from our mothers' wombs as we are born, waters that came from a lake made of melted generations, the rain of ancestors. In this private lake held in by the banks of my mother's body, I floated and grew from a seed to a male baby, and then the dam burst and on the spill of the amniotic fluid I fell upon the earth.

I am at a loss when I look back to my beginnings, for I do not know my real father. The lake behind me is a cloudy gene pool. Dharma came from the same lake of my mother, seeded by another father, and when the water cascaded into the light of the present, we rode side by side in the same stream, the same family with new streams coming in and changing the course of our karmas. We were still in the same stream formed by the family path. But the rush and push of her father's karma threw us off the course. The toxic infusion of his greed and ignorance drew Dharma, and then me, into rapids where the stones were jagged and ripped our flesh so that the water was stained with blood.

I left Ramone and went up through the country, on buses bumping on uneven roads, to Delhi, where I met Hamid Balik, Mr. Nelson's driver.

He had found Shamballa and Rajiv, Ginni's children, students. He did not tell them why there was a danger, only that there was one, and because they know that karma works with respect, they agreed to leave their studies for a small time and went to hide.

It is a slow strange river where I float, a bit lazy and unconcerned, for we are waiting, and waiting does not move any quicker when you push; it moves slower and becomes heavier, a weight. We are like this in India, waiting under the stars that affect our destiny since the minute we join our earthly stream of karma. I am floating now, bobbing downstream, and if I think revenge, it hurts my head, for I would rather swim and determine my speed. But I must wait, floating.

Georgia

And it happens in Madurai, where Nelson books just one room rather than our accustomed two, with a bottle of Indian wine and the honey of India flowing sweetly. It is the India I had wanted to imagine, but I didn't dare let myself soften into this other vision — *exotic* India, where the floors are made of marble, silken fabrics shimmer, and flowers decorate shrines to Shiva and Shakti, the love couple, deities who symbolize salvation through loving, the India that can imagine the equation between physically coupling and spiritual knowledge. Nelson. My lover. I can call him "my lover" now, and in being able to do so, I can be here, in this other, gentler India.

For four days we live the adventures of new lovers, without the cloak and dagger of mandranioxide madness, until we stop in Auroville for a cup of tea in the clean white home of Dr. Mandy Fogarty and her husband, James, nestled within the utopian community where the solar illumination of the Auroville crystal ball pulses.

Mandy extends a welcoming hand and gives us a brief orientation of the town, explaining that their temporary work stint in Mangalore had come to an end so they had returned home. They are founding members of this community.

She explains: "In Auroville, our original pledge was to work for betterment outside of the confines of race, religion, and country and join as one in peace and harmony. We believe in this still and I'm very glad that you have stopped in to see us, but I am sorry to begin as the bearer of sad tidings. Laxmi, the young woman you brought to the hospital in Kochi, died two nights ago from complications caused by an infection in her liver."

Glass shatters. Reflections of peace and harmony are strewn.

"James and I, through our work in Auroville, have been fighting against almost impossible odds, and for years have been circling, skirting around the influence of two very warped men, Dilly Willy and Daku Man Singh. They caused Laxmi to die. Also Karma's sister, Dharma. Their names only begin the list."

I had felt in that hospital waiting room in Kochi that Nelson's twin sat with us, while Laxmi, despite her virtual presence was beyond my vale. The net of my otherness blurs my knowledge of Dharma, a misty figurine, fragile bone china smashed, a subject of conversations with Karma as intimate as confession, yet in the past, a time dimension away.

A gap.

I'm cracking ... backward ... away from understanding where I stand in this. What I am a part of.... *Nelson, who are you? Mandy, who are you?*

A mess, the broken shell of a hard-boiled egg.

Mandy's voice interrupts my introspection. "I first learned of Dilly Willy and Daku Man Singh through Phoolan Daichee from the 'perfume factory.' He is a good soul *now* but he hasn't always been. He used to work with Daku Man Singh. Phoolan, from a family of witch doctors, educated in England, gained a pharmacy degree, returned to Mother India, and became a very rich and influential man when he developed mandranioxide. The basic ingredient is methaqualone and it was first synthesized here in India in 1951, a sedative-hypnotic drug that became known as a safe barbiturate substitute. You might know it best in America as Quaaludes, or as the recreational drug mandie, mandrax, or mandrake. Phoolan, as the producer of the brand Mandranioxide, unique to India, introduced datura to the mixture and found the results stronger. Datura is the plant that had once been used only in sacred ceremonies here in India. I believe you know some of this from Bernie, don't you, Nelson? We are both saddened by your brother's demise and also very grateful that you have agreed to come here to India."

I slip my hand into Nelson's and he returns my grip so that it hurts.

"Phoolan Daichee's sister married into the Man Singhs, a powerful family with connections to a series of ritual murders in the generation before this one. They were called Thuggees — the origin of the English word *thug* — devotees of the fierce goddess Maha Kali, a bloodthirsty deity whom, they believed, desired human sacrifice. The most notorious Thuggee was the present Daku Man Singh's grandfather.

"At any rate, once the families joined, the brothers-in-law, Phoolan Daichee and Daku Man Singh, were definitely operating on a different level. They opened what became one of the major drug companies in India, THG, and made a fortune when their shamanic recipes became the basis for the anaesthetics that are still used today. When we prepare a patient for surgery we use a form of mandranioxide. But there were rumours that linked the drug — and the company — to the selling of illegal organs.

"The fatal end of Shauna Daichee and the subsequent turn-around for her brother, Phoolan, came about because Daku Man Singh discovered that his wife had a lover — no 'good for the goose' here! He punished her in a horrible way. He gave her to Dilly Willy as his personal sleeping partner, and if you were to know more of Dilly Willy — the rumours fly — you would understand what a horrible punishment this must have been, for he is a gross creature despite his cultivated ways. He is known to engage in cruel perversions with women, men, children — they say even animals! The rumours were large despite the fact that Dilly Willy, the man, was known to only a few. But Shauna was Daku Man Singh's wife! His identity may have even been protected from her but she would have heard of him. She *must* have heard of him — plus the drugs that they must have had to use on her to bring her to prostitute, and the beatings ... a horrific fate!

"I was working at the time in the clinic in Mumbai, trying to monitor the outbreak of AIDS. We had an outreach program and I visited many of the brothels. James and I had been in India for many years. Shauna Daichee was famous and was pictured on many of the posters and advertisements for Indian ethnic dance. When I found her she was drugged silly and she was pregnant, about to birth, and I discovered two days later that Moona was born. She may have been forced to lay with Dilly Willy, but I have heard that his sexual appetite is not one that produces babies. She was pregnant long before! As a baby, Moona was small, delicate, beautiful, and it has been said that Dilly Willy could not resist his appeal, but I think the motivation must have been greater than a sudden and unusual bending to sentiment or compassion. Miraculously, the illogic of a miracle, he let Moona live, claiming, as you know, that he was his son!"

I turn to Nelson. His eyes are narrow slits, his mouth set, and his shoulders tight. I am disoriented for a moment, thinking it connects to me. But he has fallen down a tunnel where I can't squeeze in and, with his hand still clutching mine, I am stuck between our world and his memories. Blood ties, consanguinity, and it's a tug-of-war, as if his twin has a claim on him from the realm of death. Consanguinity. It dawns on me. Moona must be

Duma Rajpit's son! He's Ginni's brother! Rajiv's and Shamballa's uncle! The deaths that Moona is threatening Naruba with would be on Moona's own kin! The squirrelly leap from insight to excitement tumbles to the possibilities for grief.

Mandy carries on. "When Phoolan discovered Dilly Willy had killed his sister, he began to question his own slight of hand. He had been Daku Man Singh's own private Dr. Death and Daku Man Singh had sold his sister to a whoremaster! The fact that she was pregnant after such a long time of being unable to conceive, and that the man who claimed to be the father was the notoriously perverse Dilly Willy, didn't make sense. Phoolan decided to accept Moona as his nephew — that was clear, given that his sister had birthed him. He also knew that Dilly Willy had killed his sister and he understood that in a roundabout way he, too, was implicated in her death, for he had told Daku Man Singh — the loyalty between men, the alliance of their sex, the infamous double standard! — that Duma Rajpit and his sister were lovers.

"Why Phoolan could not have left it alone, left his sister some love, some beauty? This is India and it is not the Indian way to leave alone when retribution is being called for. Phoolan is an Indian man of a warrior sect, and if a man stole his sister away from his brother-in-law, he must correct the shame that she brought upon herself. Loyal to the family. Loyal to the sect. Loyal to the male. A discreet word to Daku Man Singh and Ramone Sanchez was put on the job.

"My research." Mandy hands me a book titled *Current Shamanism in Modern India* with her name, Dr. A. Fogarty, on the cover. I turn it over. On the sun-yellowed dust jacket I see a much younger Amanda (Mandy), hopes exposed.

She goes on. "Phoolan wanted to know what was real and what was made up. He was muffled within his own magic spells.

He needed an objective opinion. He came to me, a Western woman who had once interviewed him for a book.

"I was intrigued by his information. And to his credit, Phoolan Daichee became the mole. He brought us the name that gave us direction — Duma Rajpit — and from there it was easy to find the thug that Daku Man Singh had hired to kill him, Ramone Sanchez, and to chase down his fate.

"Phoolan? He 'downsized.' He renounced his position in THG and opened a humble shop in Mysore, this little 'perfume factory' that Karma took you to. He dabbled with Daku Man Singh's requisitions on private orders, provided drugs and meds, but they never worked quite the same. Phoolan was carefully tolerated by Daku Man Singh, who, developing high hopes for Moona, kept a sycophantic eye on his brother-in-law. As a man with first no son and then a weak, spoiled son with his second wife, he did not want Moona's paternity questioned. It suited him fine the way it stood.

"We have finally been able to pay enough bribes to free the man who murdered Duma Rajpit. To paraphrase the great bard, 'O wicked spite' — I believe it is our destiny to set it right. We are all involved in trying to break the Dilly Willy/Daku Man Singh stronghold, all coming at it from different angles, for we are all interconnected. It is karma.

"I would like to read to you an interpretation of karma, not the rather sugary interpretation of the hippie movement, or even a mainstream American opinion of the word *karma*. But it falls in line with what we are dealing with. Listen. 'Karma: principle of retributive justice for past deeds.'"

With this abrupt and succinct definition, Mandy, who must be in her seventies, begins losing breath. She chuffs down like a tired steam engine.

Quite an afternoon tea, as the bubble of pleasure surrounding my Nelson becomes fogged, swaddling our budding romance.

Eight

Plausible or Impossible

Georgia

Hyderabad: the safe space where all is to be resolved, where we will see Dahli, Maria, and Ginni — and Karma will join our eclectic mix once again. My world will be more organized as I research the case histories of prostitutes on file at Urban Help. Nelson and I can explore the city, falling in love.

But my insulated dream of redemption fizzles in the face of reality the minute we get off the train. War has begun. It is March 19, 2003, and the Americans are bombing Iraq. They started at six-thirty this morning.

With the headline "War!" being announced to the early morning bustle of Indian commuters from every newsstand, rickshaws pull up and surround us like a posse ringing a bandit. The front pages of an English newspaper divert Nelson from his bargaining and, as he stops to hand over a few rupees, within seconds there are pinching claws nipping at me, talking their Indian babble, trying to gain my attention for reasons I can't fathom. I call to Nelson, who relinquishes his shrewdness in trying to get a good price for a rickshaw — a game he hates to feel he has lost. Thankfully, he chooses one of the battered tin transports, although for no good reason, and we are off into the centre of Hyderabad.

"That was harsh. I didn't see you being swarmed. Sorry, but we can't ignore what's happening in the world, Georgia. Hyderabad is home to one of the largest mosques in India. America has just declared war on a Muslim nation and we are highly visible Americans. And I haven't seen another white person since we arrived. I'm used to being in wars, Georgia. This isn't a good sign...."

I grow tired and disoriented while we try to find a hotel room. Since our visit to Auroville, Nelson has seemed distracted and I am at odds with myself. The trip from Pondicherry was too long. Nelson had been in the bunk opposite, a little shelf hanging on chains from the wall, and the trio of businessmen on the two bottom levels talked on and on and on, practising their English with him, posturing worldliness, keeping me up, shutting me out. It was as if Nelson had forgotten I was there, although I'm really not clear what I wanted him to do with me at that point anyway, for it was not as if privacy was possible. But I keenly felt his disappointment with my plea for silence when I finally stepped in and aired my complaints. Then I felt bad. After all, they were only talking. I must have seemed horribly spoiled. Something is eroding my confidence and I find it hard to be as natural, giving, or generous with my spirit as I would like to be with Nelson — as Nelson is with everyone. I am hoping that here, where we can be in close proximity to the offices of Urban Help, I can establish some sense of routine, even if it is only for the week we are planning on being here. Hopefully he, too, will relax a bit.

Finally, we find a hotel room, the fourth choice on a round of room viewings. This one doesn't smell of damp carpets. We move into gear, making phone calls and sending an email back to Bernie to tell him where we are.

Nelson turns on the television. All the rooms that we've had recently have had TVs, for even here in India there is that droning background of chatter and canned laughter, but we agreed, on my prompting, that the immediate environment is where we would search for clues and news. I am firmly prejudiced. I hate the background jabber of a television set.

I turn down the volume in order to obliterate the scream of the needle-nosed war planes.

Nelson turns the volume up again.

I sink into the armchair near the window to ignore him by looking at the sign opposite: GUTS GRIT AND GLORY — POLICE FORCE! On the billboard, policemen with the insignia of Hyderabad wear green, white, and red greasepaint.

"Why are they wearing face paint, Nelson?" I want him to come over to me.

With a backward glance out the window and up at the sign, Nelson turns off the television with the remote and sighs. "To announce their allegiance to the great gods of cricket. They've made the Indian flag with their faces painted that way. Let's go meet your friend, Nur."

I wonder why he calls Nur "my friend," but decide not to challenge it although I feel slighted, as if he is diminishing my reasons for being here, as if this is just my hobby or pastime — chasing prostitution around India.

We leave our stymied space to walk into the bustling streets of Hyderabad, Nelson fiddling with his phone. The bright orange of blood tangerines appear dull ochre under the shade of a grey tarpaulin and it draws my attention to a man who ducks out from the overhanging canvas and into the exposing glare of mid-day. It is Moona. He snuffs a *bidi*, hoists his dhoti between his legs, and swings into stride, heading into the traffic with the hop of a practised hare.

I know Moona's story. I have this knowledge, this power over reality, but rather than being reassured by the sighting — after all, it means he is still following us as planned — I am irked, as he reminds me of the reality path I am on with Nelson. We seem to have meandered away from the romantic exotic backdrop of India — as it appeared when we first became lovers — and now are too much back in "the stressful India." The lustre has worn off the illusion of love; I feel like I am Nelson's partner but coupled only through chance. We are back on the mission, more tied in with sad and sordid pasts than present happiness. Perhaps both Nelson and I have played the respite of a romance out.

Nelson, squinting at his BlackBerry screen, lifts his eyes too late to catch Moona, the rabbit going down the rabbit hole, as he reads to me — "*Thug — follower of thuggee; ritual murderers centred in Madhya Pradesh in the last century.*"

Nelson is unwilling to stay on topic when I try to lead the focus to "us." He says that my fretting bothers him and he makes a plea for a broader perspective. Our conversation wends its way back to Moona and his familial ties and then back to the great big topic — this "war." I run out of comments. Nelson leads the way, but after an estranged silence he suggests a brief overview of the surroundings from the famous towers of the Charminar as we are about to pass by them.

From the top of the south tower we look down on the mosque where we have been told that ten thousand men are gathering to pray. The bazaar radiates outward from the Charminar, an ant-like flow of business as Nelson worries on. "With the prayer meeting in the mosque, I am more concerned about the large influx of Muslim devotees than I am about anything else. I am also concerned for you and your safety. I have a second sense, Georgia. I developed it through the many years that I was covering combat situations. If there is a Muslim with a grudge against America, here in Hyderabad, right now, and based on our immediate experience — isn't that your gauge? — who would you target?"

Two veiled women with a group of open-faced, garrulous men glance at us, but as I smile into the women's amber eyes I realize that I have no idea if they are smiling back or not. They stare at me longer than they should, an expressionless stare, then look at the men, who look away from us and hurry them down the long, winding staircase.

Urban Help is less professional, more easygoing than I had projected. I settle into a wicker chair in the offices, glancing at the posters, notices, and brochures on the bulletin board encouraging participation, health, and proactive measures. Dahli, Ginni, and Maria come in from the residences that they have been given nearby, excited by their good fortune. Maria is going to Urban Help's school half-days and we speak of this before we hug and cry about Laxmi. We all have tea and meet another one of the staff, Fatima. I try to engage but I stray, for I am not thinking of her but of Nelson, who has gone off to talk with Nur, who entered with his hand extended toward Nelson and then scurried him off with barely a salutation toward me. Thinking of Nelson, I am sad. Our wonderful closeness has become so seemingly bland, as quotidian as any old marriage — no direction, open-ended, meandering toward nothing substantial.

I tell Fatima that I have seen Moona and she says she will record the information in the log they keep on the case. Then Dahli, on hearing Moona's name, occupies Fatima's attention until we are led into another room for an audiovisual presentation.

I come out to join Nelson outside the office after watching a short video about Urban Help and the various programs that they sponsor. He had left after the first few minutes, apologizing, saying he was feeling claustrophobic and needed to catch a gust of air. I find him leaning against the building, pensive, handsome, and I am glad when he slips his arm around my waist and we decide to walk back to the hotel. We go into some of the pearl shops and he buys me a necklace. We watch the sunset reflected in the windowpanes of the top floor of a narrow, crooked building like two bloodshot, glassy eyes and laugh at our both seeing it as such. We are close again, softened for a while.

But back in the hotel room, blasted with the overflow sound of a nearby television tuned to a Muslim station, I become annoyed at the intrusion and something in me turns over, a stomach flip of nausea. Perhaps it's the slippage of caresses that makes me feel tired and slighted, not necessarily by Nelson but by India. It is all I can do not to punch the ragged Indian pillows and bang on the floor so that the person downstairs will turn down the damn television and it will not be so confusing. Perhaps it is the stress of moving from room to room, always inundated with solicitations, far away from the familiar, and this overall neverending *test* of India. I'm not bearing up well. I want to be awake; not in a fake fuzzy glow of impermanence! This is what India does for me. It makes me sleepy but I can't fully relax to fall asleep. I have become a dozer.

I snuggle closer to Nelson and he responds. The night folds over us with the macrocosmic war having begun in the big world but a microcosmic peace beginning in my little damaged personal world. I have Nelson. I will be all right. We fall asleep curved together and, distracted by his closeness, I am able to ignore the blare of the television below.

We rise to find a note slipped under our door: *Meeting at Urban Help. 12:00 hours. There will be a car waiting to take you at 11:30.*

Nelson slips the note in his pocket. "I believe the television has been going all night long. Sounded religious. I wonder if the man below knows that there's an American man and woman in the room above him."

He is persisting in this attitude that there is a personal conspiracy against us. This is where we differ. It is not my problem, this war. I begin to doubt him again and then dislike myself, as well, for feeling duplicitous. My attempts at communication, at recognizing, understanding, and pleasing start with the first bell of the morning. It starts between the two of us first, and then we become a team and it gets easier, as the struggle is between us and India. We are self-confidant individually — I am, Nelson is, and India's identity is poignantly strong — but there is a damned dynamic as we mix and match at odds.

As I step through the hotel's front door, a white car, a Hindustan Ambassador, from the opposite side of the street does a quick U-turn to pull up in front of us. The driver hands us into the back seat as Nelson goes on about foreign policy and I try to zone out, catching the sights, learning from my eyes.

He interrupts my musing with a tap on my leg. "Where is this car taking us, anyway? We're heading further into the old city. We're not going toward the office...."

Nelson, alert now to the immediate, brings my flagging attention into focus and as we each collect ourselves a voice from the front of the car speaks in English through a microphone so that we notice the glass partition between the back seat and the driver.

"If you protest too much, you will protest no more." The click of door locks competes with an educated accent. "There is a bomb under your seat. I have my finger on the trigger and I'm not afraid to die...."

We are told as children not to get into a car with a stranger and, realizing that our bodies are small and easily overcome, we follow directions and we never get in that *bad* car; but as an adult, to find myself inside the trap, the first rush of danger comes with the feeling that I have disobeyed and will probably be punished for my misdemeanour. But I *had* protected myself. I am with Nelson and he will take care of me. Still, my body shrinks as I hear this voice, distorted and nasal like a robot. My head swings to check where Nelson is. My bob bounces against my cheek and there he is beside me, appearing, alarmingly, as insubstantial as I feel. He is recognizable, familiar, my man, from my world — but diminished as if there is a lessening of the juice in his veins rendering him too soft to be of support.

We are trapped.

This is not an ordinary Ambassador but a firmly locked strong steel can with windows that stay up when the buttons are pressed. Nelson is as ineffective as I at releasing the door locks. We are trapped and I strive to remember how to breathe.

The seats are low and cushy. If I prop myself up on the front edge, I can see through the glass into the rearview mirror to the source of this disembodied movie script. The back of his head, his neck needing a shave; his ear with a translucent edging of vermillion; the pristine pressed white shirt collar; and past this — my heart forgets to beat — hands, gloved. It is a cinematic moment where all eyes, all the brown eyes of the invisible Indian audience, are trained on this car careening through the streets of Hyderabad in spurts that jerk, purposeful stomach-throwing jerks. But with all eyes tuned in to our channel, I have lost my lines, the script is forgotten, the characters ill-defined, the prompts aborted, and my role embarrassing and botched.

The voice natters on — our punishment to listen, filtered gravel gibberish — as Nelson bangs with his shoulder trying to open the door.

"Don't jiggle too much! It will go off! I said there is a bomb under your seat and I am not afraid to die!"

Nelson freezes. I begin to shiver and can't get control of it; I am now afraid that the motion will upset something.

"You are like so many foreigners." The disembodied voice continues to rasp in a conversational tone. "I know you well. You think you have the answer for us, the third world, Indians. And you do. But we don't have to wait for you to give it up. We use you, as you study us. We go to your universities, we copy your ways, but we are not seduced, as you believe. We aren't fooled."

I see him now, reflected in the oblong mirror, cocked eye-brow, arrogant dissimilation of a fanatical intelligence. He is young.

"Surprise, surprise! I know your lies!" He makes faces at me and, hypnotized by his insanity, my attention is held so that my body balances back into its proper tasks, breath, blood, flesh, with systems performing in harmony with one another. Now accustomed to the queerness, I am again somewhat resilient. Shifting into observation, I recognize another element in the monologue, above the subject — his delivery. Between bursts of vehemence, the man is grinding his teeth.

"Tell us what you want," tries Nelson. "We can negotiate."

"Oh, my, my! What a surprise! You want to negotiate. Americans? You little people, identified by your country. Hiding behind a nation, a nation with a fool for a fatherhead!"

The Ambassador scoots, stops, inches, puts forth, jerks, jams brakes, squeals tires, acts out. *Where are we?* I look from Nelson to the outside, where the colour and clash of India is spookily silenced. He recognizes my unspoken query, pulls me closer, and nudges my side where I feel the BlackBerry in his hand. I glance down to notice that the light is blinking GPS coordinates — and although they are meaningless to me, I think Nelson knows what he is doing, tracking our progress.

Our driver motor-mouths; the ride for us becoming a drawn-out, excruciating, carsick, stuttering, snivelling dilemma. We are only ears — a weird confessional, imprisoned priests.

"I am a member of an elite class, a caste that dates back to the thirteenth century. We are warriors, and over many generations the secrets have been kept within our families. We have married into our caste to safeguard the knowledge — none of your nosey, American, chit-chattering, trying-to-figure-the-Indian-out. We have our secrets and you will not break our system with your

prying and poking! We are elevated beings, a higher caste than
Brahman. Exclusive. Selective. *Dacoits* they called us. Bandits,
thieves. But they were wrong in calling us a low caste, for our
practice is far higher...."

Props and patter, I think; Nelson has a grip on this.

"You try to uncover our operation but we are paramilitary,
if your limited imagination can fathom this concept. You dare
to try to push your way into our ways. You are American, self-
centred and *fucking* stupid."

These small threatening increments. He is telling us to back
off something. Fine, I will do it! But I don't know what he wants
from us and I say nothing. I just sit there and say nothing at all. I
think, *Nelson, the madman's right; we are stupid*, but I can't speak.
Frozen. Scared.

The robotic voice stops for just a moment as the car turns
onto a dirt road. Before us is a large red-brick wall.

"Kali and the double-edged blade of the Daku Man Singh
family passed from my grandfather to my father and so on down
the line until it will be passed to the last Daku Man Singh. I
have studied the rituals of magic, shamanism, and the wild
man."

Bush and grass brushes the undercarriage of the car until
we stop. The driver opens up a piece of folded paper on his
dashboard and there it is — a small pile of white powder. The
sinews in his neck grow ropy as he draws his chin in like a turtle
and holds his forefinger to first the left then the right nostril to
inhale. He smiles smugly at me from the rearview mirror.

"Do you think I was born yesterday? You are thick. Barbarians!
Maha Kali is not from your world of killing for money. She *likes*
to drink the blood of her enemies. She *loves* the strength of the
blood. The iron! Maha Kali is not an ordinary goddess. She is
sublime. Do you know what this means? *Sublime?*"

Nelson is trying to do something with the BlackBerry, and from his look I understand this is my job — to listen, riveted to the eyes of the man in the mirror, riveting him.

"The sublime is beyond your understanding. It is outside of the scope of your philosophy. It is like the words of Hamlet: 'There is more twixt heaven and earth than is dreamt of in your philosophy.' The Prince of Denmark. I am an educated man, Americans. It is 'dreamt of' that catches me. Maha Kali has many incarnations. My great-grandfather killed about a million people, right near here, for Maha Kali. He and around five hundred of his followers were arrested. It was an Englishman that spearheaded the cleanup."

Nelson leans into me and whispers something but I don't hear because his door has sprung open with a whack and I watch as he is flipped over onto his belly with his head being pressed into my lap. It is strangely intrusive despite our intimate relationship to have him struggling for air with his head painful against my groin, so heavily is it being pushed down. From my throat comes a squawk as I feel Nelson's body relax across me, leaving me alone with this horror, and as he slumps, I see his attacker for the first time. With a green garbage bag over his head, little holes cut for eyes and a yellow scarf holding it in at his neck, he is pressing on Nelson's back, rubbing under his T-shirt. Then he rips at Nelson's palm, prying his fingers apart. I squeal as I watch the toss from the door and the smash of Nelson's BlackBerry on the car hood. As I squeeze back toward the opposite door it flies open and a damp palm presses onto my cheek, hand covering my mouth as I stare into the dilated pupils of our driver. There is no appealing to these eyes, no soul, no conscience, so that his masked humanity bears as little resemblance to a man as does the garbage-bagged head, yet, helpless, I swoon into this horrid man's grasp and with an epinephrine rush I start to go down and away.

But then I slow to a quiet spot in my head. I remember many years ago when an Indian magician invited volunteers to a stage to be hypnotized. The Pasha had spoken his magic words and then began instructing his hypnotized players to do silly things. When it came to my turn, the hypnotism hadn't worked on me — either that or everyone else on the stage was also only pretending to be hypnotized. And this stray thought prompts me to play dead. Just as I had pretended to be hypnotized then; this time I pretend to be unconscious. As I still myself I wonder about Nelson and hope madly that he might still be here with me, but I can't look toward him without blowing the cover of my supposedly drugged awareness. I must distance myself even further, for I experience intense discomfort as I am hauled out by the arms, the driver's sweat dripping onto me and a foul breath of *bidis* and *feni* mixing in with the sour odour from his underarms, pressed close to my ears. It takes more control not to vomit than to remain limp and I have to swallow a rising in the back of my throat as the driver horks off to the side.

I hear a door opened ahead and what I am aware of is Nelson being dragged in front of me, and then the bright red on my inner eyelids, the unavoidable inner glow from the bright Indian sun, changes to black as I am bumped over a threshold. I hear a flashlight click on as the glimmer registers again on my inner lids. I maintain my passive posture, knowing that this is how they light their way as they haul their seemingly thought-less cargo through what must be a long corridor — smelling damp, brushing on me now and again so that I fear spiders, a picayune present worry winning unrealistically against a greater possible future demise. I feel the space opening as the claustrophobia of walls, close and old, is suspended. The air feels bigger, stiller.

The driver places me on a hard floor with a modicum of care although the impact makes a "whoosh" sound as my breath exhales. They plop Nelson beside me and I almost blow my passive posturing when I feel his body jerk as it feels as if a kick has been delivered to his poor prone helplessness. I must try to see what I can but, afraid of my ruse being discovered, I allow only a narrow see-through slit so that my lashes fringe my vision. The man with the garbage bag yanks at his scarf and draws off his mask, but as his face is turned away from me, and through the filter of my lashes, I see little.

The men haggle as they leave. Their voices and the light from the flashlights recede into the distance of the long hallway as the room grows dark. I feel in the absolute blackness and find Nelson's warm, soft arm. I need him to be here for me. I want him to be awake and as alive as I am more than anything I have ever desired. As my hand slides down to his wrist and then his fingers, I feel a gentle double squeeze.

I hear him softly, barely audible, "Shhh!" Then a bolt slides and metal clunks. We're locked in.

Karma

We all share a papaya with many seeds, fertile and full. The priests in Goa would eat the seeds of the papaya before they played soccer so that they would be stronger men, so that they would win their game.

Nur tells an amazing story. Moona is not the son of Dilly Willy, but the son of a beautiful woman and a famous dancing man, Duma Rajpit, Naruba's brother, Ginni's father. We are all here together waiting for Memsahib and Nelson to join us. Ramone and I got here first. Keeping company with a goonda. The two women, Dahli and Ginni, they have come in this morning to welcome us to the Urban Help headquarters. Nur,

Fatima — we all smile to know that Moona is Ginni's brother, the father of Dahli's child. Ginni accepts the information like a gift and then says that this could make right all that has gone wrong, like a blessing. Even with Ramone, the man who had killed her father, she is gracious, but I can see that she is stretching her patience. I can tell, for the flesh on the top of her cheeks, just underneath her lashes, twitches. Not a small movement but a ripple.

But my smile sticks in my throat when I hear that Laxmi has died, half-formed beginnings that didn't bloom.

The seeds of the papaya will make a woman lose her baby so that it falls from her body like a wrinkled brown mouse with eyes that will never open. Women eat the seeds, black with filmy veils like sperm on dead marigold seeds. We make a garland of marigolds in India when we marry and the bridegroom wears this around his neck. Papaya seeds kill babies before they are born and make men strong to win their games.

Urban Help. We are fitting together, somehow, but our day and our stories are interrupted when a car right out front of Urban Help bangs into a tree while we eat our papaya and *BOOM!* The old cooking woman rushes about, upsetting pots, and twists the gas valve from the cooker to OFF as we sit there with our papayas and stare at one another. Wide dark eyes. Indians on a mat in a courtyard when a car explodes.

We go to see it; a car blown apart, frizzled fringes and melted plastic stinking up the air, the lines weaving and wobbling around windows and there is no back seat, just a hole that has spread deeper in the street. But how bad the car looks — this is not the worst to see — on the front, tied to the little side mirror and smoking, is Memsahib's shawl with the embroidered dragon. Dahli wails and wonders why it is there; always she has to talk her way through things — everywhere there is worry — and we are also frightened that something else might explode so we watch over our shoulders and walk with gentle steps.

In India there are always people and when something goes wrong there are more people to come and see who has had the bad luck. Nur, the boss, is into the business of solving the car explosion so he moves the rabble away from the door of the office where they have come to find out what has happened. They go back to ponder the carcass of the white Ambassador. We are called to sit around the big table in his office like we are a team of experts. He pulls a piece of paper from an envelope that he says had fallen through the mail slot, "delivered by hand" about an hour earlier. He hadn't bothered to open it, he says, but now — he tells us to be quiet. He reads the letter that stops our hearts:

Did it scare you? Are you afraid? We are powerful. A pair alive for a pair alive. A pair dead if the prostitutes are not by 17 hours at the shop of Mustaf Ben Ladin, Sultan Bazaar, end of Mahipatra Road. No men!!! Come only women under veils. Ginni and Dahli.

Nur and Fatima cannot make Dahli be silent. She is going too fast with her panic. She is mad at someone and yet we are all innocent as we can be with plans to murder in each of our heads. We all want death. Retribution. We want the bad guy to die so that we can survive. Dahli wails on and her shrill accusations are confused, so we try to think where we fit in, but all words stop when Nur's hand reaches into the brown envelope and comes out again, holding up and opening. In it is the cracked lens of a pair of glasses.

"We didn't expect this. Nelson assured us it would be all right. I'm surprised Dilly Willy — it must be him — has opted for this. They're foreigners."

We say nothing. We are not important now and stay still when Nur is on the telephone. Fatima holds her finger up — *hush* — and he talks. When he is finished, he speaks to us like we are his team. But I remember the deal in the note. He wants to trade two women for the two foreigners. Dahli had reason to wail....

"The American embassy is not answering. The world is distracted right now by a war and it's Thursday, the day before Holy Day. The square around the mosque is covered with white-clothed Muslim men. I passed by this morning. The gigantic chandeliers are now uncovered. This doesn't usually happen until Friday, the day of prayer. Prayers have been ringing through the night. I heard that there is unrest. There are papers circulating saying that the white capitalists are to be blamed.

"The Charminar is close to Sultan Bazaar. All women in the vicinity have to be veiled. It is why they have told us to have the women covered. They will not be noticed. It is overflowing with the devoted and I have heard that the atmosphere is not peaceful."

I follow Fatima's look toward the front door and remember the fuming flag, Georgia's shawl. Nur's computer begins to beep and he turns to the screen as he talks. "There is an email coming in. It's from Nelson! From his phone. I don't understand. It's just numbers, no more."

Nur taps on his keyboard and waits. "It's returned. Says 'sender not available.' Why have we lost reception?"

"What are the numbers?" asks Ramone, who has been still, quiet.

"18.751 and 78.345, nothing more...."

"I know what this is." We all listen to this man, Ramone, now. "It is time to use a goonda and a sailor. Those are latitudes and longitudes. I remember that Mumbai, at the harbour, was 19.3 and 74.2. I think we've found where your friends are kept hostage.

And someone transmitted the coordinates to us, so chances are they are still alive, unless the loss of a signal was a fatality. We need a map of Hyderabad."

Nur is back on the keyboard again, but not for long. All is in emergency time, fast, and he twirls around in his chair. "They're at Golconda Fort, in either Rani Mahal or the Harem. That section is closed for reconstruction. No tourists, in the works for ages, so probably no workers either."

"I'm the goonda. You get me in and I'll be at the exchange when it happens. But I need a gun."

We all jump at this. Ramone checks on the computer and tells us it's 13:45.

Nur picks up the note and reads again. "Ginni and Dahli. Under veils."

Ginni looks worried but Dahli is beside herself. "More to do. Save them. Why me? Take her. Take Fatima! Save them, you tell me, but you don't know what Moona is like when he is mad. It is Moona who is chasing for Dilly Willy. *Moona!* He will not be calm. I know Moona. *Moona mad! Moona surprised!* — and how can this work?"

Then I am distracted by a scrape as Nur opens his desk drawer and brings out a gun. A very modern gun. Even Dahli stops. Ramone takes it from Nur and turns it over in his hands. I can tell that he, too, is surprised by this gun.

Nur turns his screen toward us and shows a map. He talks straight to Ramone. "It's a taser gun. I will show you how it works. This is the Golconda Fort. There is a strange sound phenomenon in Golconda. In some parts of the fort you can hear the words spoken many rooms away. By the same fact, in some rooms there is a muffling of sound greater than in a pile of felt. The Harems were muted rooms. The journey to the fort is about an hour. If we are to hand over the women at five, they should be at the fort just as the Light and Sound Show is beginning. This is a tourist show with an audio system, eerie music as actors and dancers put on a play. The noise will further obliterate any wrongdoings in the Harem. Ramone, you must go."

I want to know what is supposed to happen with me. I want to help, but when I look at Nur or Fatima they look away and so I listen more.

"Let me see that map again." Ramone traces with his big fat finger across the map on the screen as Nur frowns. "I believe it would be better to enter from the rear. They will undoubtedly be watching the entrance. But it looks like there's a passage from the Raja's quarters through to the Harem. I'll take it. This is my chance to begin to be an avenging angel. I will not forget that Ginni, the daughter of the man I killed, will be coming in through the doorway with this beautiful woman, Dahli, who is brave above all. I want to be sure that everything's under control long before they arrive. And Nur, Fatima, all of you, thanks for your trust. But there is one more thing that I need. A goonda does best with a man by his side. Let me take Karma in with me."

This was what I had been waiting for, my place in this. I am not so sure about the gun, though, but the burly man rises from his chair like the first strong spurt of water from an early morning fountain. I follow like his right hand.

Georgia

The transition from being held prisoner in that car to being locked in that basement went without struggle only because we both were playing at being unconscious. Had I known, or had time to project, to imagine where they were putting us, I think I might have tried to scramble away somehow. I was more scared of totally inconsequential things during that haul from the car — soiling my clothes or getting surface scrapes — than deep thrusts of blood-gushing violence. The menace pulsing from the driver was the worst, so strong that it made my mouth taste like burnt plastic, but, somehow, my realization of self seemed more overwhelming than the bizarre reality of being lugged from a car down a corridor to this dark, damp place.

A new fear takes over when the lock thuds into place as I think they will hurt us horribly or kill us unless we escape. Nelson is angry at them but also with himself, expressing his sense of failure at doing what he set out to do, at keeping me safe. He is intent on this but I assure him that it is nothing to do with him. I am glad that he is here, to help me deal with being in this black space. I would die from fear without him. Ransoms, bargaining, all of the possibilities that go with a kidnapping seem near to meaningless in the face of being shut into such darkness. It is deathly quiet and cold, not like India, not even like imaginings of the underworld. I can't stop shivering. Nelson holds my hand and we whisper, sitting up on the floor, afraid to move far, afraid they will come back and find us awake and even worse things will happen. We whisper to try to figure out how to overcome the ending without saying what that ending that we each fear is.

Nelson's hand is squeezing mine and I bond to him, tight as a knot, with the warm cupping of palms together — an indescribable togetherness existing alongside of the other, inescapable awareness — of no light, no water, no idea of what we are in for. We stay together, hand in hand as we rise and even when we feel about, inching forward with our hands out like blind people, we don't go far from each other. I am not sure how long we move this way, discovering a wall, creeping along it with fingers on the cold stone, looking with no vision, moving as slow as snails with a methodical thoroughness, hoping that it will reveal something simple that has become something nearly incomprehensible — a way out. Then the horror floods back with a rush at the sound

of someone fiddling at the door. We move quickly now, shoulder
to the wall, my hand drawn forward by Nelson's and we lay back
down, as still as bedbugs just before the light goes on. The door
is opened and from the end of the tunnel a pin-size point of light
comes closer. I fear a greater, deeper darkness as the light comes
forward.

And then illumination with the first words. "Memsahib, we
are here to help you."

Karma. My guide.

He is with Ramone, a stranger, but we know his story and
there is no time to waste on knowing too much. They have
water, a flashlight. Karma explains to us where we are but the
narrow beam shows more accurately the stone prison we are
in. He tells us what he knows, events — past, perceived, and
planned. We learn about a taser gun. It is not long before we
hear feet descending stairs and then — at the *other* door to our
subterranean dungeon — the scraping of what sounds like a
heavy log.

I brace myself, lying on the floor with Nelson, playing dead
again, while Karma and Ramone wait behind the door.

A grunt as rough upon rough slides. The wooden door
slowly scrapes inward as light enters and we are caught in the
beam. Nelson lies closer to the door than I, a barricade between
the flurry of action and myself. He jiggles against me as a cry
signals that a woman has been pushed toward us and has fallen,
and then another jumble, a riffle of added confusion — *another
person pushed?*

Then Ramone calls "Moona!" My eyes disobey my resolve
and pop open, but only to be blinded by a blue zap from the gun.
With my mind racing, I must wait for my eyes to recover in time
to see Moona convulse and then fall. A second shot and a man
who came in behind Moona does much the same twitching in

an agonized, spastic way and then collapses, unconscious, with another heavy thump. We all stay suspended in silence for a few seconds as if we have become frozen by these brilliant cobalt flashes. Then, in the deep yellow afterglow, I begin to register that Ginni is on the ground near Nelson. Dahli, as well, with her head covered by her arms. They look like mounds of voluminous cloth for they are both wearing burkas with the veils unhooked to drape back upon their shoulders. As Dahli looks up it is as if there is again that commanding, enlightening glare like the moment our eyes met in that boxcar.

Ramone's hand with the gun drops to his side.

Moona lies on the dirt with his head flung back and his face covered with blood. An Indian man in a kurta is bent forward on his knees, utterly still.

I have no time to even shiver, for Dahli has sprung. She seems to launch in the air and she throws herself at Ramone and hits him again and again, screaming at him in her language, but then she trips in the tangle of the burka so that he catches her, bends on his knees and cradles her swathed in the cloth like a baby. He holds her arms tightly against her sides, wrapped in the cloth of the veil and talks to her in Hindi.

I think no woman could escape a man if she is wearing this cloth.

We are told that we do not have much time, for Moona and Gurda will both awaken within ten minutes. They have been stunned but Moona looks like he is dead with blood around his nose, covering his chin, and staining his shirt collar. Something must have gone wrong. Karma had told me that there would be no bodily harm from these guns, just a short period of unconsciousness.

The sunlight is briefly blocked as Nur comes in with two other men, and as the human pieces of the pandemonium are picked from the dirty floor, I see that the second man is Gurda. Involuntary shivers finally break free to tremble through me. I am freezing, chaotic within my body. Nelson handles me, passes me forward, past the bodies, around the sights, dirt coagulating with deep dark blood, and I become scared, paranoid really, outside of comprehending anyone else's needs. All I can do is cling to Nelson and get out and into the air.

Nine

Breach

Georgia

There are no prayers from the mysterious Muslim below and we sleep curled into each other until ten. Neither of us seems able to wipe the previous day off without discussing it, so with tea and an orange, like any normal couple might discuss a movie watched the night before, we review the scenes.

Nelson is a gadget man. Yesterday morning he had slipped the GPS, BlackBerry (a very advanced technology and just new on the market, he says), and the small camera into their respective pockets in his combat pants. He has a habit of recording his photographs with the exact longitude and latitude of their location, his private way of organizing. He had punched in the GPS coordinates, the numbers, on his BlackBerry once we had arrived at that awful destination and then managed to hit the speed dial for Urban Help before the man with the garbage bag mask grabbed and smashed it. That was how he had let Urban Help know where we were. To think I had thought him paranoid in his preoccupation with intrigue. Now I can count my lucky stars; because of Nelson and his ingenuity, we are alive today.

My shawl had been in my bag, here in the hotel room. It was stolen, as was Nelson's spare pair of glasses. It's an uncomfortable thought, for it means someone was looking through our things, probably when we were at Urban Help. We go over the plot again and again as Nelson tries to figure out how we managed to walk into such danger. He says that he blames himself for the incident, that he should have been more alert. I can do nothing more than praise his performance, telling him that he exercised great presence of mind, in the Buddhist way, with mindfulness. It wasn't his fault we were kidnapped. He had, in fact, saved us. But for me, admittedly, the most important aspect of his support is that I can trust him to help me. I know who he is. He is on my side.

Our conversation doesn't solve anything other than to make me feel calmer about my relationship with Nelson. I believe he really cares for me. But when I ask him to sum up how he sees us moving forward, his answer is less sympathetic to my feelings than I would have hoped. He says we should be more wary and proactive.

At the office, they, too, have not stopped churning and rehashing. Mandy and James arrive from Auroville. When Ginni and Dahli come over to see us, salutations, congratulations, and hugs fly the rounds with a bright realization of the goodness of being alive permeating every revelation.

We have many small logistical inquiries, most of them centred around the gun, which we all examine with awed interest. Although it looks like a gun, apparently it's not. It's an NLW, which stands for non-lethal weapon, a form of taser, designed to give off fifty thousand volts of electricity at a range of up to fifteen feet. A peaceful organization like Urban Help is only allowed weaponry that is prophylactic, protective, or used for other peaceful purposes, although in this case a non-lethal weapon might *not* have been adequate protection. Moona could have arrived armed. But the element of surprise made it seem likely that it would work.

Dahli gets upset during the gun discussion, conducted in Hindi and English, and in the midst of the staccato conversation, Fatima explains to me that Dahli is chiding Nur for having exposed her and Ginni to danger. Really, they had been lucky that everything had fallen in the order that it did and that they had been pushed well out of the way before Ramone had to fire. The blood coming from Moona's nose was nothing more than a nose bleed — not an unusual reaction to a taser shot, we are told. The men stayed unconscious only to recover ten minutes later, but by that time they were sufficiently restrained. As it happened, Ramone was the one who clarified for Moona the convoluted web of relationships, including his parentage and new family connections.

Then there are things to tend to as Nur calls Nelson to help him out and it is just Fatima and I left sitting in the office. She asks me how I am doing, praising my bravery, saying that she can better understand Nelson's involvement because of his emotional commitments, but for me, as a woman, to accept such danger, is admirable. Although I thank her for the sentiment, I defer. It's not as if I knew I was going to be kidnapped — I would not have agreed to put myself in any real physical danger. I explain to her that it's Nelson who makes me feel safe in this volatile atmosphere, and without him I would not be appearing such a heroine. When I politely demure to her praise, I am surprised when her response seems rather cool as she says, "We are at a serious crossroads and it's time to fill you in on an even broader picture. There seems to be much that you are unaware of...."

But as Nur returns with Nelson, both of them looking very hard-nosed, Nur signals abruptly to Fatima to stop talking to me and I sense she has been put in her place. Nelson avoids my eyes when I look over to gauge his reaction to Nur's abruptness but we seem to now be in meeting mode, so I just listen to Nur, who is now talking directly to me.

"Moona is now with us, no question — I've filled Nelson in already. It wasn't hard to convince Moona of an option to being the son of Dilly Willy. We showed him pictures of his father, Duma Rajpit, taken just before he died. It was effective. He was responsive. There was a lot for him to take in — including the knowledge that he has a daughter who is HIV positive. Yes, Maria. A sad fact of the sex trade. He was happy that he could see them both before he left this morning.

"Out at Golconda, we got Moona to the van before we called the local authorities. Gurda 'came to' believing that he and Moona had somehow been intercepted as they were about to pick up the two of you. He thought that Moona had escaped. Gurda was taken into custody for questioning. We never really know whose bribes are more powerful, but I suspect that once the story filters back to Mumbai, Daku Man Singh will intercept and Gurda will likely be released. His reportage to Dilly Willy will verify the version we want them to believe of what had happened at the fort and Moona's role in it.

"Moona met with Devanand Daku Man Singh this morning. His alibi as to why it all had screwed up is well-supported, so it went smoothly. That was your captor, by the way, Devanand Daku Man Singh, the driver of the white Ambassador and Daku Man Singh's son."

I am becoming confused, so I interrupt. "I thought he didn't have children...."

"When Shauna Daichee was killed and Moona born, Dilly Willy offered to come up with a new wife for Mr. Daku Man Singh. He promised to find him a wife who was both beautiful and fertile so that the Daku Man Singh family would continue, since his first wife had failed to produce an heir. Dilly Willy did more than was asked, and he found a 'donor' of sorts, undercover, for this new wife. Devanand's father isn't Daku Man Singh. Dilly Willy arranged the stand-in, the false paternity — who knows who, doesn't matter — but Moona verified that there were rumours. Mr. Daku Man Singh doesn't know this yet, of course, and Daku Man Singh is not going to *like* this once he is told the truth of Dilly Willy manipulating his 'progeny.' I believe we have enough on Dilly Willy to break the rather perverse bond of loyalty between these two men. Even bad blood runs deep.

"Devanand Daku Man Singh, the son, is a mixture of influences. He comes from a spoiled and privileged class that is notoriously politically corrupt. Devanand has access to the underworld through his father's business and Devanand owes Dilly Willy a lot of money. Likely drugs, cocaine or heroin.

"Moona was supposed to have a few people to turn over, dead and alive, to Devanand Daku Man Singh. Photographs were to go back to Dilly Willy of the prostitutes as proof of their deaths. The 'two foreigners' were to be delivered to Daku Man Singh, alive, until you told him what he wanted to know."

What's that? I look to Nelson to see if he knows, but he won't catch my eye. He seems sunk in his own head, distracted by his own personal take. I am distressed by his aloofness and wonder what has passed between him and Nur.

"When you arrived in Mumbai, Georgia, and began snooping around the brothels, Daku Man Singh was focused on his pharmaceutical company, THG, currently under investigation for a product that he is trying to bring onto the American market. He is proposing a crucial element be added to the 'cocktails,' the drugs that Westerners use to fend off AIDS. Daku Man Singh has been arranging a deal with the University of Indianapolis to sanction the use of mandranioxide. There's a spotlight on Daku Man Singh and he's got a lot of dirt to cover over, ethical filth, not to mention prostitution, child pornography....

"Daku Man Singh is on the wrong path. There's not much that happens in his empire that he isn't made aware of, but in your case, he did his research and came up with the wrong results. Morgan, Miller and Sheinmann. Bernie Morgan is the champion — documentaries, ethnographic research, exposures. Daku Man Singh thinks you're on his trail to uncover the mandranioxide scams and his involvement in the illegal sale of human organs. He thinks that's why you're in India and he's afraid of what you might have found out. Nelson arriving as your photographer sealed it for him. Especially since Nelson's brother had been a victim of an 'accident,' made public at the time by Bernie Morgan. The war has come at a good time for Daku Man Singh to take advantage of the confusion."

My head spins.

Nur continues. "It has to accelerate. We are asking you to invest yourself in your ethnography in a way that goes far beyond the definitions you have learned for this type of research, Georgia. I have already discussed this with Nelson. The code name for our plan is 'human sacrifice.' Not to a deity, but to a cause — the betterment of a people who need help. Many of them women.

"You know of some of the deaths — Norman Finigan, Karma's sister Dharma, Shauna Daichee, Duma Rajpit, and Laxmi, whose initiation into the sex trade we tried to intercept ... but were not able to. This is just your list, a foreigner in our India. We Indians carry longer lists of loved ones who have fallen to these two very evil men. We may have a way to turn around this sordid pattern if you will both help us. We can prepare you. We will warn you. But you will undoubtedly, once again, be made very uncomfortable at some point. The only thing we can be reasonably secure in expecting is that you'll be in it together should either of you agree to help us. They see you as a unit by now."

Ten

Morbid Monkey Bars

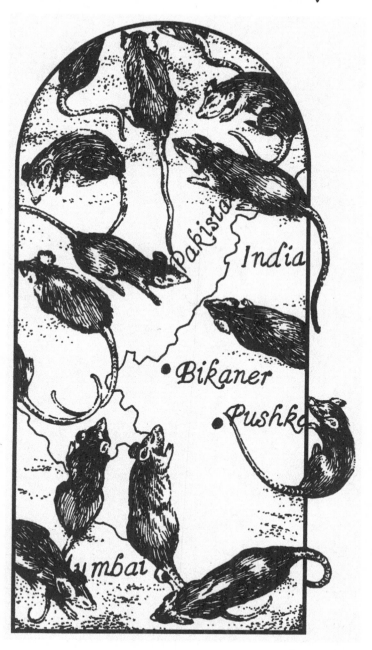

Georgia

In the hot afternoon, as Nelson and I walk back to our hotel, kiosks along the way hawk baubles and I buy a small basket, thinking of children I know back home and little Maria here in India — bracelets and barrettes. I don't want to think of what Nur has hinted at, which I know is danger. There are pretty dresses hanging in tiers, layered with gauzy flounces, inexpensive, one hundred rupees, so I buy one for Maria with red and yellow roses on a fringed, crimped border. I make purchases to clothe the little girl from the inside out — lemon yellow socks with ruffles at the ankles, underwear with rows of pink lace, and Chinese slippers that are embroidered with silk threads. Nelson soon yields to my frivolity and offers his opinions, calling me over to other choices. I take stock of the moment as we browse on, further into the alleys of small market stalls with their tinselly offerings — silver cups, oils and incense, candles, flowers, spices, *kumkum* powder, and a variety of beaded, embroidered, bejewelled fabrics. I smell sweat, perfumes, sugary sweeties on braziers, chai, and *bidis*. I am enchanted with the red stains from pan on the yellow ochre earth. I breathe in the happiness of my gifts and relish how lovely it is to be alive. I think of "ethnographic research" and the pompous sound of the words.

I am changed. I want to defend beauty, to justify life to fit everyone's needs, to facilitate all that is good and generous, and to be brave enough to help these people. I had come to India with a vague idea, an idea of "furthering things." Now I am walking with a bunch of pretty little-girl presents, with a man whom I am beginning to like more and more. I might almost be in love. It seems an unfortunate time to be asked to be a human sacrifice.

I say that I can't do it.

This, of course, precipitates the biggest confrontation that Nelson and I have come to. I want him to believe that I am a brave woman who stood up with courage during our recent trauma. I want him to feel proud of me, but I cannot, with good conscience, agree to have my life managed from an outside perspective toward an undisclosed encounter with what? I am not as brave as he thinks I am, as Fatima believes, as Nur wants me to be. I am a woman who wants to love, to help them all, but what they want of me is too much. I can't do it.

I put up an argument. I find that I am forced to by Nelson's constant rebuttals. His brother, his twin brother — he asserts as if he had lost half of his identity — died because of these men, Dilly Willy and Daku Man Singh. He has come to India to attempt closure to his brother's death and he has found himself closer to being effective than he previously imagined possible. He is committed. Whatever it takes. He is willing to be crowned by this phrase, "human sacrifice," with the overriding belief that he will come through the victor, and that I, too, will reign proud by his side, his royal empress, the imperial woman. If only I can trust him, trust the plans that Urban Help has put into place and think beyond "me" to envision a larger idea of life, one that is linked to others, because personal happiness is not fully possible if we are this intimately aware of injustice. It goes on and on. I feel guiltier with each moment, ashamed of myself for not being sufficiently resilient to spring back up and into action.

But I cannot do this. I do not have the motivation. I value my perspective, my sanity, my life more than his love and respect. Yes, if it is to be one for the other, I'm not there. Nur has said that if one of us is in, then we both are; they see us as a couple. I want to hear *only* that they see us as a couple, and if we are a couple, then I, too, should be able to influence Nelson as he so aggressively needs to influence me. But it has never been said — in sickness or in health, rich or poor, until death — none of that has been confirmed. I feel it has become a contest for affection between me and his dead brother, and I say as much.

It stops Nelson's barrage of influence. He looks sadly at me. I have come to know him and believe that he is not so hard as to be mean. He is determined, stubborn in his Irish way. He states once again that he has his reasons and wants to be of service to a larger good. This is why he elects to go with their plans. He tells me not to worry, that he understands my hesitations and he wants me to be authentic. If this is who I am, he will try to find a way to connect with my decision. But we will not speak of it again, he says, and I can easily tell that this is a command, not a request.

I avoid speaking now, for I am close to crying. We walk in our individual personal silences through the noisy public market. We eat in a restaurant and then go back to the hotel where I shower as he reads the English newspaper. When we lie down, we inhabit a cool space where lovers leak tears that drip from ice. His back to mine. Mine to his.

Karma

My life, my karma, gathers different people into my stream of being. I am back in Mumbai. Ramone, too, is in the city, although we travelled from Hyderabad separately. Now I meet with Moona. He is smart, a survivor. He is also liking to be a better class, a move toward more important people. He says "international crowd, first class," but he will have to wait to declare his conversion. Our liaison must remain secret until all is accomplished.

Moona dominates the conversation. He tells me, "The Daku Man Singh family — they are real thuggees. Our heroes as kids were the dacoits; we were in love with Phoolan Devi, the beautiful raven-haired woman as fierce as any man, and the old grandfather, Daku Man Singh, was our very own thuggee!

Devanand talked about him with pride. The pride of a dirty secret."

The pride of a dirty secret. But when you don't tell the secret, the pride grows too big and the swelling in the head hurts me. Moona is incurably boastful. I, too, have tales to tell but he won't slow down long enough to listen. He smokes continuously. I am glad that we meet outside.

Inside, my head wanders and I think of my mother who killed her husband, the man who was not my father. I return to this thought every day and wonder if the knowledge of murder is the karmic thread that ties me to these people, some who have been criminals; or is the karmic thread Dharma's untimely death? Murder seems like a negative tie, more like a knot that is tangled and tight. To respond to the suffering of a virtuous sister is surely a cleaner tie, a good strong knot with an order to the making of it. I cannot easily abandon the image of my stepfather dead, and my part in it.

Moona brings me to life when he says that Dilly Willy must die and Ramone is to carry out the deed.

"Ramone was always the meanest, loudest goonda. A barbarian. Always with the whores, rough, not nice. We all stayed clear of Ramone. Shit, man. I went into the fort expecting to secure the Americans so that Devanand could take them to his father but I was ambushed and woke up to Ramone. I couldn't believe it — Ramone! What a fucking shock. This huge blast and when I awoke, there was that goon.

"Devanand believed me completely when I met with him later at the fort, but he was afraid of what his father would say. He's weak. Too many drugs. We got Gurda from jail and we came here to report back to Dilly Willy and then to Mr. Daku Man Singh. That scared the shit out of me! His office has always made me feel like a small boy. I might have been shakier but when I brought in Ramone for proof, and Mr. Daku Man Singh heard how Dilly Willy betrayed him — right away, he ordered his death. First thing!"

Moona and I sit in the seclusion of chunks of cement on the banks of the Mithi River. No one can know that we are connected, so we crouch hidden by the industrial waste of Mumbai, close enough to the centre, before the shanty towns where the waste becomes fetid, before the pigs dominate, ruminating in filth. I don't tell him that I, too, want to kill Dilly Willy and then leave all of this shit. I am not a man like Moona. I want to be a nice man but now I play a role. Ramone, Moona, and I, we must meet as men do, with smoke and reserve, in dirty places. We take stock of what we have done and what must be done next, and this is why I listen to Moona's story of what transpired this morning in Mr. Daku Man Singh's office with close attention. If I am to change my karma, I must be aware.

Moona brags on. "Har! It was like Ramone had plunged a knife in Mr. Daku Man Singh's heart! First time the knife thrust in — Ramone, he pushed it in hard! He told Mr. Daku Man Singh that Dilly Willy had deceived him when he said that Shauna Daichee was unfaithful. He told Mr. Daku Man Singh that on the night he killed Duma Rajpit, he had learned that Rajpit was a holy dancer and had not had sex with Shauna Daichee — that they were dancing partners only! Ramone pulled me forward and said — *dramatic, Karma, like a big movie scene* – 'Mr. Daku Man Singh, look at this young man. This is your real son! Moona is not the son of Dilly Willy, but your son, and you have been deceived by this crow as I was deceived by him!' Ramone was strong in his telling and Mr. Daku Man Singh, he sat there and listened. He looked at me, too. He thought that I was his son now and so he looked at me hard and I was afraid he would see that we were lying to him. He would not dare kill me if I was his son. Har! Just like I wished when I was a little boy! When Mr. Daku Man Singh heard from Ramone that with the new wife that Dilly Willy arranged for him, he also arranged a man to father her children, the knife twisted deeper."

Moona and I hang about for the day discussing the reasons things go wrong and about the curse of being men. We are working with blood, with who is who in blood and who is who when blood is poisoned and who is poisoning the blood. Mr. Daku Man Singh gave to Ramone one more goonda job and I will ask him if I can help him this time as well, for I know the face of Dilly Willy and can identify him. I was a good partner for Ramone at the Golconda Fort, he has told me this, and I can help him. I might not wield the knife but I can add my courage to the deed. It seems to be my role, to be there, to witness, to understand the horror of retribution, and when just retribution is dealt with a knife, there is no doubt that it is called revenge.

Moona tells me that there has been another order issued by Mr. Daku Man Singh. It, too, was given to Ramone, and I jump when I hear that the plan is to kidnap Nelson and Memsahib. Mr. Daku Man Singh was not so immersed in his private emotional concerns to forget his primary purpose. He is intent on diffusing the Americans, believing they are the root cause of his troubles with the acceptance of mandranioxide. This knowledge scares me, for I understand that poor Memsahib must suffer more. When Moona goes further to say that he has told Urban Help already and that Nelson has agreed to being in this danger in order to trap Mr. Daku Man Singh, I am afraid again. I think Moona moves too quickly with his change of loyalties. He reported back to Urban Help before he met me today.

If Urban Help knows the danger, and if Nelson knows, surely Memsahib, as well, must be preparing herself for this trouble. But I do not think she can do it. I do not think she is that strong or clear. She is not awake and thinks mainly from her own needs. In relation to all that is happening, she has no deep reason to support their plans, to offer herself up as this "human sacrifice." She must love Nelson very much to agree to this.

Nelson is tied into his karma by family. This is the strongest tie. Memsahib is not so lucky. She is a little lost and perhaps always will be until she finds her true family. It is not her fault that she is weak in her purpose. She has no past karma to urge her forward. She hops about. It would be better if she found her family. She, too, might feel this need and that might be why she is attaching herself to Nelson.

Georgia

I believe there is something within the psychology of a woman that feels disgusted by war or killing of any kind. In the same vein there is the inclination to nurture, so I am wrestling with reconciliation. I want to be generous toward Nelson and his thoughts, to pay respect to his radar, his more experienced sense of what is dangerous in foreign situations, and with him to accept the challenge to go further with Urban Help and their plans.

If one of us is in, they said, we both are. But what are we in for? What is the plan? What is supposed to be happening? Nelson has put his foot down with a masculine stomp on discussing this option that is floating between us in lieu of living harmoniously, and that leaves me in the dark. I am grateful to him for his protection so far. I know that he has felt a manly necessity to take care of me during all that we have been through. Nelson is a good man and I trust him despite the fact that there is one large unresolved difference between us that has become our "unspeakable." The code name "human sacrifice" has disappeared from our conversation, and for now I must ignore this. Miraculously,

we maintain a truce, at least convivial enough to continue to
coexist.

Our scheduled time in India is drawing to an end, with only
ten days left before we are booked to fly back to America. We
have Hamid — Nelson's acquaintance, the one who hid Ginni's
children — as our driver now, a safety precaution I am told. We
make a loose itinerary, deciding to visit Rajasthan. My research
into prostitution seems no longer important to anyone. I have
the feeling that I have been relegated to the doghouse and that
this directionless meandering is part of my punishment for not
agreeing with Nelson about our involvement in this "human
sacrifice" scheme, whatever it may be. It is not so hard to realize
a shunning, but for me it is damn difficult to confront the issue
when I feel that with doing so, I may lose Nelson forever.

India. We travel through the centre, Madhya Pradesh.
We pass through Agra for a brief disappointing tour of the Taj
Mahal. Each day of driving turns up a number of casualties and
overturned trucks become morbid monkey-bars dominated by
urchins. I watch as an oncoming Tata slowly careens off the road
and skids on its side in the dust. Boys are running to the spectacle
before it stops, still tipped. They cheer as if a circus has come to
town. A man crawls out the window, a stiff jack-in-the-box, then
another, and then a third, whooping with his arms above his head
in a victory pose. Most wrecks don't look as if they experienced
such a positive outcome. The cars are the worst, crumpled and
pinched with gaping broken shells. Buses lie littered with broken
sacks, spilt grain, and smashed oranges. After the humans have
gone for the spoils, cows graze on the leftovers and then goats
leap into place to clean up after the bovine aristocrats.

I am not feeling comfortable with the free-flowing happen-
stance of the route that we are now on. I have become invisible
in some respect. I am not sure of my place when it comes to

planning. I began this trip with single-mindedness that turned into a series of karmic links that led me to understand larger issues than I had originally targeted. And although, admittedly, I have made friends along the way and had incredible encounters that went beyond my previous personal experiences, I feel less aware of who I am and why I am here than ever before. The echo of this "human sacrifice" will not leave my head. I am unsure what is driving Nelson forward now, how committed he still is to Urban Help and whether he is holding his brother's demise out in front of him to guide his karma forward, as before, or have we indeed managed to realize a comfortable co-existence.

Last night, Hamid said that he has organized a camel safari in the Thar Desert once we reach Bikaner, two days away. My first reaction was that he had overstepped his bounds. He shouldn't be taking initiative for what we do. But then I thought, loosen up. This sounds nice. It might help me to feel closer to Nelson.

On the route to Bikaner, we stop in Deshnok at the famous rat temple, Karni Mata. There are kiosks outside of the temple grounds where *prasad* is being sold, the little white sweets that look like fudge — one of Nelson's indulgences since chocolate isn't always available. We leave our shoes at the entrance gate along with all of the devotees, step up and over the door jamb and we are surrounded by the scurry and bustle of rats, small rats, although now and again a big one attracts an exclamation. Three rats hang from a prayer flag that is tangled in with a necklace of marigolds. They intertwine, their tails forming art nouveau–like graceful curves with curlicues of flowers and gauze.

"A storyteller died," begins Hamid. "He was the son of a devout man, who prayed to Karni Mata to bring again to life, please, his beloved son, the storyteller. So Karni Mata go to Yama, god of death. But Yama, he is happy to have this talented soul, the storyteller, in his dark place and he want to hear stories.

Karni Mata try very hard. She work all her powers and — yes!
— she bring the storyteller back to life, but she not make him
man again, only get him to the rat life.

"Rat spit is sacred spit. Eat rat spit from the Karni Mata
Temple and you have good fortune! Look now, low bowls of milk
on the temple floor so that the rats can drink. Rat spit slips from
rat mouths and falls back into the milk. The milk left from the rats
make *prasad*, to eat by the devout as they worship Karni Mata."

I like this brush with the bizarre and Nelson seems more
relaxed, less self enclosed, more open with me. As we start to
get into the car, he even stops to photograph two women and a
young girl who have bundles of twigs at their feet. Hamid points
them out to him.

All of the fabrics for their garments — the sari, *choli*, and the
children's dresses are a deep cochineal red with russet and phthalo
green accents. Their faces are darker than the Indian brown skin
and studded with gold piercings — noses, lips, brows, and ears.
They have tattoos on their cheeks, even the two little girls. The
woman bends to pick up bundles larger than each of the children
and places them on top of a roll of cloth balanced on their heads.
She winds her own cloth tighter and adjusts it on her head as she
bends from the hips, keeping her arms straight to scoop up the
massive bundle that is left for her to carry.

Nelson hands the camera to me and helps the woman lift the
bundle up and on. She straightens from the knees to face him and
then turns and walks into the desert, her hands raised in prayer
toward the hot sky as she follows the little girls already on the path.

"They are gypsies," says Hamid, "from the Thar Desert."

Bikaner is a small desert city in northwestern Rajasthan, one
hundred kilometres from the Pakistani border. The newspaper

headlines that morning as we left Pushkar — Jihad Mushrooming in Incidents of Violence at Pakistani Border and Perils of War Reporting — are echoing in my brain as we look for lodgings. *How close is that border?*

Although we arrive in Bikaner late, Hamid brings us to a great hotel with painted ceilings, large palatial rooms, and the trophy collection of a hunting Maharaja, stuffed and hanging on the honey-coloured walls. There is a fireplace, decorated with a relief of lapis, malachite, and jade, above which the skin of a tiger is splayed. His gaping mouth hangs slack in mute appeal to the gazelle staring blankly above him and whose glass eyes, in turn, reflect the blue glass bulb above the carved wooden bed.

I know what I am missing. Peaceful, safe seclusion. I need the space to be me without being strong and stoic, and I need a partner. I need Nelson to look directly at me. He has been avoiding real intimate conversations. I wonder if I am being tricked. I don't have the mettle to bluff with my life. Is that what I've been doing? I am, frankly, growing afraid that I may be just a pawn in his game, and his grand allusions to my being his queen have, on his part, been abandoned.

Over morning chai, Hamid reads the *Pakistani News* — in Urdu, I am told — and Nelson reads the English version. Hamid's paper is fatter. Both frown. I look at the pictures, upside down, across from Nelson. This lopsided news exposure parallels our personal views of this war. He reads what he is able to get his hands on from this outpost and accepts it straight up, trusting that right is being enacted. I am not so willing to place my faith in possibly biased reportage. I'd rather see it upside down. Maybe I'll catch a hidden truth.

Pakistan's border looms close and there have been skirmishes; people killed last night, so close. Hamid had seemed nervous as he made the arrangements for our "private safari," not registering with the police department where legally a record must be kept of tourists on outward-bound adventure tours, especially as there is a war. "Best price," he says to me when I question him. I feel we are compromised even further since our association to Urban Help, with all of their international associations and repercussions. We'll be sitting ducks in the desert — white, fluffy, obvious, and vulnerable. I see this quite clearly now but I am loathe to confront Nelson on it for fear of a reprimand. I am worn down, too tired to fight, and really, I'd rather trust in his goodness.

When Hamid leaves to fetch the car I try to express my concerns to Nelson, but he just says "Don't worry baby, we're fine. I'm on top of this." I allow myself to be appeased even as it shuts me out. Hamid arrives with a furrowed brow to drive us to the embarkation point where we will meet our camels and he will leave us to our guides, the sand, and border proximity paranoia.

Camels are my favourite animal! I hadn't thought so before meeting the dromedaries — they're not really camels, for they've just one hump — named Mata and Raju, but now I am in their thrall. Raju is hooked to a flatbed wooden cart already piled with sacks and stuff. Mata is saddled with a hard, wooden-frame saddle, posed bent with knees curled under like a sleepy-eyed sphinx. A cluster of men gather as we are given the option to ride in the cart or on the camel. I want the camel ride. I am determined to give this a try, but looking over at Raju, who stands, I hesitate, for a camel seems so high above the ground … and with such wobbly knees!

As I climb on Mata, Raju looks down his nose at me, I'm sure of it, not haughtily but as if he can't quite see past the slope of the pierced bridge of his nose where the harness is looped to steer.

His top lip curls up, a sneer with the look of an old man trying to balance a monocle. It's easier than I thought, getting on, but then Mata tips forward onto his knees as his hind legs straighten and my head whiplashes as he rises to bashfully acknowledge the cheers of the men and children clustered to watch the white lady.

Nelson sits on the bundles in the cart, turbaned in a rusty length of cloth that is really my travelling bedsheet. His dark glasses, hooked on the wire rims of his prescription lenses, suit his features. Perching atop my camel, I feel glamorous. Loping at such a height is a grand, glorious sensation. The lighting is intense, unreal, like an extended backdrop for an exotic photo-op. It is a biblical setting where all is placid and quiet, with not a sound to contest my exuberance except the casual banter of the three camel men and the creaking lurch of cart and saddle. Visually pure, there is nothing to look at other than sand, dry stubble brush, and the vista of rolling dunes. I alternate from riding straddle to riding with my knees drawn up. Nelson sits cross-legged on a patchwork sack, squats on the wooden planks, dangles his legs over the edge, or leans against bags of camel food, the bulk of the load.

I am experienced by the time that Mata kneels to unload me and Nelson takes his turn as a screen star with the sun lowering behind his silhouette, but he is stiff and sore within ten minutes. When Mata lets Nelson down, the poor camel's back legs hook up, crisscross, and he bawls like a baby with his under-lip flapping and trembling, gasping and belching while the driver unthreads the knot, literally untying the camel's legs.

Later, with Raju unhooked from the cart as the handlers arrange to prepare our food, I sit close to the camel's head and draw. Lying on his side, with his legs curled under him, relaxed on the warm sand, the woolly dromedary sleeps while I trace his outline, develop the shadows, and race against the dying light to hold fast to the perfect peace. I'm no longer concerned.

My reality check, the immediate. I feel safe. All is well. There are no borders visible. They are non-existent irrelevancies. The men cook a dinner of rice, lentils, and chai using dry brush they have gathered. The fire just supports the one pot and the meal is passed from person to person, each taking a scoop from the pot with our chapati. We have a shot of *feni* at the end in tin chai cups. Nelson has two or three. He seems to need it. He is not as easily able to convert from his accustomed comfort level into our camping mode, it seems. He spreads out his bedroll and lies looking up at the stars, immersed in his own thoughts.

As the men converse while cleaning up, a shape appears on the horizon, moving toward us over the sand dunes, and I have to interrupt his reverie. It is a magical sight, a group of women with their saris dusting around them. I can hear their bangles jingling from this distance.

"Nelson, look, gypsy women!"

With bright cloths lifting and settling with the stir of the evening wind, they make camp about a hundred yards away. Their presence compliments the serenity of the landscape as if they had been called forth to accent the scenery with a brush of beauty. They form a congregation of colours, ranging between violet and orange so that they seem in tune with the last rays of the setting sun. A feeling of sadness comes over me as I recognize the domestic arrangements and remember how far I am from a comfortable quotidian round.

A little group steals over to our camp. They appear curious, sneaking sloe-eyed glimpses while they talk with our camel men, then return to their group. Two come back and lay down bundles by our fire, which the handlers blow back from dying embers to a neat blaze. The women place a pot on the fire, add leaves and powders, and accomplish their cooking in a few minutes. The scent is seductive and relaxing. They lay out a long rouge cloth, patterned by quilting, and roll out two cylinders, which they place at the centre. There is a readiness as if a blessing is about to be given. They signal to our camel men, who come over to squat by our bedrolls, and through gestural sign language, we play a kind of charades, hoping to guess what they are trying to tell us.

"What do they want, Nelson?"

"I think the women will massage your feet. See, she is doing it to her friend. Want to try, Georgia?"

"Only if you will. It smells so nice, I'd love to, really. And it can't be that late, nothing else to do...."

The petite pretty women fuss over us. Nelson is nervous, probably his stubborn set-in-place side balking at the unexpected. The women arrange us on the quilt so that we are lying crown to crown, with each of our heads slightly raised on the rolls. We each have a woman at our feet. We are like a religious offering.

My gypsy treats my feet by turns, washing them with a warm cloth and then beginning to massage with the warm oil. I relinquish my tension to their slow, gentle movements — tiny fingers caressing my soles, my road-weary feet. I divert from the pleasure to attempt to analyze the scents — lavender, with a deeper aromatic undertone, then there is chamomile, cinnamon, and frangipani. The last whiff is sweeter, almost sickly in its pungency. An undercurrent of valerian....

Eleven

When Eyes Open

Karma

He has done it. Ramone did it. The scarf cinched, the throat choking, and the snake died on the head of the rat he swallowed. The act of vengeance a sufficient reason to strangle. Then Ramone beheaded him. One sharp slash. Dilly Willy is dead and I celebrate his death and pray that he will move down the ladder of karma to awake as a dog that is kicked because he is such an evil cur; even that is too good for him.

This strangling and cutting was Mr. Daku Man Singh's instruction. It is a horrible sight, so I look away from the place where the head fell to the floor; but I cannot resist the gruesome draw and turn back to look again. I see Moona bent with a rag in his hand, closing Dilly Willy's eyes with the cloth covering Moona's fingers, a thin sheath between his hand and the lush lashes. I watch Ramone collecting himself with solemnity, coiling the bloody yellow scarf, slipping it into a plastic bag, wiping the knife, doing what has to be done so that he can leave Moona and I alone in the room with the dead man. We know what we are to do. Moona and I, delivery boys, out through the back door and then Moona will bring the head back to Mr. Daku Man Singh.

My feet drag limply as if I have lost the use of my legs. Kohl leaks from my lids, oil seepage stains, black as grief for the sister I lost to this evil man, strangely savage though he was clothed in sophistication.

Moona is able to speak. "It's strange. This is the head of the man who I saw as my father for most of my life, and I must carry it in a gym bag, in a fucking gym bag! Har!"

I am sick. A head. A body. I am sick, crumpled. Now I have lost my legs, body, arms, tongue. Moona asks what is wrong but I cannot tell him. I cannot help him as he wraps the head in the cloth and puts it in a plastic garbage bag and then a second plastic bag, for there was blood sticking on the cloth, a stain still

growing. He wraps it in the black bag and it becomes a big ball
and then in another bag and it looks as if it has gone away — but
it will linger forever, blood seeping through dreams.

Then I speak, a croak, as I catch my breath. "This head, in
a bag — in a gym bag — and I see the hands of my mother,
Moona. I see death from the hands of my mother."

"Hold on. Hold on, man. Hold on. Your mother's not here,
man."

Moona, too, had a not-father. We are brothers now, moving
quickly to leave this dead bulk on the bed, with the weight of the
gym bag for Moona to carry, for it was his not-father, false kin,
distorted beginning. Moona is doing the work. Labour of death
belongs to the son as labour of birth to the mother; but my poor
little mother, labour of birth and death.

I talk to him, keep him brotherly company, as he wraps. "My
sister died because of Dilly Willy and she died because her father,
who is not my father but as evil as Dilly Willy, sold my sister to
Dilly Willy. My mother killed this evil father and I was there. I
helped my mother murder this not-father. I lit a fire, piling junk
on top of his dead body to make him burn, and the stench of the
smoke has not left me, the smell of murder. And so I know this
murder of a not-father that you speak of — this head in a bag, in
a cloth, in whatever you use to cover a dead head!"

"Take it easy, man. Sorry, man, sorry. Here …"

"Don't touch me! Stand away and just listen to me for a
change! I think, is it finished? My evil not-father is finished. But
today I see him again in Dilly Willy. Believe me, they are the same
— these white slippers and the grease of my father, they are the
same — and I wonder if today it is finished, and the answer comes
as clear as the fog that has lingered in my head since her death.
The mist continues to roll over my mental landscape and the only
part that is finished for sure is Dharma, my baby sister. She is gone.

"It makes me weak. I am weak now. Weak and empty. I am clear of the karma of my not-father and Dilly Willy. I am not unhappy. I am an empty man. I have no happiness but I also have no sadness. I have lost someone that I carried in my heart and yet I see that Dharma's death is likely — *still!* — not avenged. Karma cleared once when my father died. It cleared again when Dilly Willy died. We go now, your dead head in hand, and you will meet with the man who is above Dilly Willy, for we learned it is not Dilly Willy but Mr. Daku Man Singh who generates the evil pulse. Does evil go higher than this? Will I learn that the gods are responsible?

"Moona, my friend. You have done wrong. I have done wrong. We are really the same, aren't we? Yes, Moona. I, too, am goonda. I helped my mother to kill her husband. I am sorry but I can see this does not disappoint you; you see how we are alike."

Georgia

The room is dim, but whether it is dawn or dusk is uncertain. I smell women, the odour of monthly bleeding. Paddle toes! Start a stretch. My arms feel a rush of warmth, not unpleasant, human and soft. My legs prickle. My neck is sore, the old writer's cramp. Look left and right.

The room stirs on a wave of cochineal red silk, kohl-rimmed rapid synchronized flutter of eyelashes, hennaed hands rustling. Faces — purplish with gold highlights. How to move. I battle inertia, fighting upward toward movement, but I slip backward as I try to go up.

I let it go, the urge to move, and lie still. The air smells watery when I close my eyes and inhale to steady myself. When I open them, I focus with an inane sense of delight.

Scalloped white plaster with arches and alcoves. Quilts of white cotton with white cotton bolsters and jewelled caramel pillows. There is a large amber glass window with a white gauze curtain embroidered with tiny men falling from broad-leafed trees. Two holes in the thick white wall, a circle glazed in gold and a crescent moon glazed in turquoise blue, mix their cascading beams and colour the white cottons a viridian green. Above, ruby glass baubles are suspended with candlelight wavering in each of the acorn shapes, breeze disturbing symmetry.

Dark purple women in crimson saris twinkle with mirrors dotting the fabric in starry formations. They watch me. Ceremonial. Their lids drop over dark brown irises floating in white milky pools. On a narrow wooden table between us there are steamy pink glasses and little cakes decorated with golden foil. Enchanting.

Where am I?

Does anyone speak English?

Where is Nelson?

The flutter of saris begins again, and with righteous ritual a glass of ruby-tinted tea is raised to my lips.

I think of Nelson and it makes me smile. The women back slightly away and then advance with caution.

"Gungar. Gungar, Parvati!"

I disconnect again. Muffling as if swaddled in wool, I can't breath deeply. When I move my head I feel motion sickness. I am lost. I want to go pee.

Then it all shatters like a daydream and I yield to the desire to fall backward.

"Try it again, Mandy!"

"Frankincense!"

"Why isn't she responding?" *Nelson.*

"She's small. It took a lot more out of her than it did out of you." *Mandy.*

"I thought you said it was harmless." *Nelson.*

"Place a drop under her nostrils."

"What is this, Phoolan?"

"Myrrh."

Myrrh. It is a word with such love. The time has come. I open my eyes to glimpse tiers of people staring at me as if I am the game that they are watching, absorbed. But nobody claps. I come out further, as if on a stage with the lights so bright that the audience disappears but I know that they're there, so I smile for them, panting with relief and exhaustion.

Then, abruptly, I recognize Mandy, hustling people, shooing them from the room as if she is rounding up her brood. "Well, we'll leave you now, Nelson. Catch Georgia up on what's been happening in her absence. Dinner is at eight."

I want a bath and there is a tub. This is a nicer hotel than we've been used to. Nelson talks from the other room as I soak. "Can you guess how long you were out for, Georgia? Thirty-eight hours! Phoolan said it was an odd reaction."

How long I was out. *Why* was I out? My hair feels silky under the water as my fingers comb out the shampoo. I have hair that is healthy, my body is strong, I am not sick, and I count my blessings. I am alive.

"He'd never seen it quite like that before. You woke before you were supposed to — while you were in the care of the women. Then when they broke in to get you, you went back to sleep."

And it strikes me like a slap — *he* let them take me! I was part of the plan, this "human sacrifice," even after I said that I would not be! He had asked me not to bring it up again and then he just continued. He's so matter-of-fact now. *But you put me there, Nelson! I didn't want to partake. I said that I was not willing, remember? I never said "I do," remember?*

Nelson comes into the bathroom, bringing me the cream rinse from our travel bag. He appears to be such a thoughtful man....

"How are you doing? Still wobbly?"

I answer not to his question but with an assertion, needing to reiterate my own resilience. "I'll be all right."

"I'll wait for you in bed."

And what will you do with me there, Nelson? Betray me again? Pretend? Put a knife in me as I nestle into the warm curve of your belly under cool sheets after hot sex, counting my blessings, glad to be a woman?

I let him know: "No, Nelson. No bed. How could you let them when I said I couldn't do it? No bed, Nelson!"

I'm not refreshed. I'm more tired than when I first awoke. I dry to his silence. I defer my judgement as I slowly towel and then slip on my light cranberry dress.

I will not be mean, Nelson. I won't hurt you.

"You must have known, Georgia. You must have known that I couldn't just drop this. We weren't talking about it, but you must have known —"

"Nelson, I knew like LSD slipped into my wine! Or poison! I thought we were a couple. Nothing confirmed — trust! We had toasted and looked each other straight in the eye, but you had poisoned my drink. You forgot the meaning of a 'toast' — that we drink the same draught, that I am *safe* drinking what you give me because we drink the same drink."

He has changed to me, no longer handsome; I see his sloping chin, gaping mouth, dulled vacancy. In sweaty-lidded India I was paired with this man? I fielded the askance look of Indian women, the clutching of beggars, the giggling commentary of children, and the loquacious come-ons of men falling before the seduction of modernity because I went to bed with this man? I have spent significant time dirty, tired, confused, deflated, and disgruntled. I admit now to doubting any love for him.

"No, I didn't know, Nelson. I told both you and Urban Help that I couldn't do it. I was clear. Nothing fuzzy. I was clear and then I was disciplined. I shut up. I didn't go over it. I didn't bring it up again. I trusted. I even let go of my curiosity. I didn't ask what *you* were doing. I trusted! I let you be you, with respect and no questions, because I was determined that I would not act like a prying wife because I didn't need to. I trusted you!"

I have never seen a man this closely. Closer than a kiss. Suffocating closeness.

Nelson's stunned look switches to retaliate. "And I, like any man with a mistress on the side, separated my love for you from my other, more emotional entanglement. I came to India to avenge my brother, not to fall in love with you! The love happened, yes, but it had no effect on my original purpose. I had a larger vision than the immediate impression of you, Georgia Quercia. I was seeing through two eyes, my sight converging to form a bigger picture. There was my immediate sense of you, warm and like an animal, real, with warm-blooded love. But then I would be swirled, twisted upside down by the hand of fate — the scarlet hand of fate, the hand that has blood upon it and blood within it. The blood that is held in by our skin. And I saw another version of myself mirrored by life.

"Have you ever seen someone's ear when the sun is shining through it and it glows like an independent life, more magnificent than the entire rest of the body? More poignant, more beautiful, more wonder-full? Bear with me please, Georgia, I want you to understand the entanglement, the responsibility to avenge my brother's death in a manner that would be effective to the ongoing health of mankind. This, for me, was like seeing the sun through an ear — a miraculous certainty brought about by the chance alignment of events. A sign from the flesh, from our corporealness. The sun shining through that ear! That ear was attached to you, Georgia. There was no way to separate you from what we were doing — what I was doing, Urban Help, Bernie Morgan. Yes, we are all in on this...."

Nelson is sweating for me. "I'm sorry, Nelson, but I was in your hands and you threw me up in the air with no real idea of where I would land." I shrug my shoulders. "Nice way of putting it, the ear story, but not good enough."

A shiver runs through me. "I don't want to have to say no to you, Nelson. Make it good."

He looks at me with that long look that he has passed my way so many times before and continues. "The facts, then. Not about me or you and what we think or feel. Just facts. What happened.

"We put in place as many safeguards as possible. All of the women, including the ones who massaged our feet in the desert, are devotees of Karni Mata, in an incarnation known as Devi, the prime goddess of the Shakti cult. They are the women whom we first saw near the Rat Temple. Maha Kali, the goddess worshipped by the Thuggee cult is *also* an incarnation of Devi. Each of these fierce incarnations of Devi had practices that involved drinking the blood of enemies. That night, in the Thar Desert, the women, devotees of Karni Mata, put us to sleep."

I am not so exhausted that my lip cannot curl upward nor so unaware of our dynamic that I cannot feel the ugliness of my sneer. "Blood-drinking devotees of Karni Mata put us to sleep...."

"The Daku Man Singh family are still thuggee. It's a little like the caste system and thinking that Gandhi corrected it so that within the Indian social structure the caste system doesn't exist any longer. But we've seen that it is still very present in the social hierarchy of contemporary Indian society. This modern man, Mr. Daku Man Singh, brought the thuggee philosophy into this century, updated the obsessions and prejudices.

"Hamid arranged our capture — one that would be convincing to Daku Man Singh. Our introduction to the Rat Temple wasn't because Hamid was feeding our curiosity and bringing us to a rather unusual tourist attraction. Hamid was introducing us to *the women*. Do you remember as we were leaving the Rat Temple that there was a woman and two younger girls — Hamid called them 'gypsies' — who were trying to load the wood onto their heads?"

"Do you think I am foolish? I couldn't have been able to see the meaning in any of this! I don't want to leave you, Nelson! I wanted it to be good. I did a good job. As much as I could, in the only way I could, *not knowing*...."

Nelson moves to hold me but I shake free of him as he tries to explain. "We were also hoping that it might help to dispel any fear, should you come to, as I understand that you did. Did you recognize the women?"

I breathe to slow down my reactions. If I am open to what he says, perhaps it will not be over. I don't cry. I try to stop my being and listen to his side, so I answer him.

"No, it was far too psychedelic. What was the oil?"

"Mandranioxide, of course, suspended in an infusion of aromatic herbs and valerian, a relaxing herb. They had to use it. They were pretending to be in cahoots with Daku Man Singh. Once we were captured, we were tested to make sure that we were sufficiently 'out,' and then Daku Man Singh had us photographed in our 'last throes' supposedly, sent the photographs to the media and then put the word out that it was a jihad capture of two American journalists. It was not all a safe charade."

"Thank you. It was not safe!"

It's all I can think about right now. Audience over. "Where is my bag? I want to find a change of clothes."

I can't seem to get away from the idea that there's a big camera up there watching us. Well, go ahead and shoot on, but make the angle flatter, the script more meaningful. I am beginning to accept what I look like without makeup. Soon I will be able to leave this theatre and go home.

Karma

Jagniwas Island, the home of Maharana Jagat Singh the second. *Octopussy*, James Bond movie. Famous palace on the Lake Pichola, and we all say goodbye.

Phoolan joined us in Udaipur, where Memsahib and Nelson had been brought. It was Phoolan and I who broke through the door. We rescued Memsahib! At least so it appeared.... We overdid it, though, for the *haveli* was not so well built as we thought and when we battered in the door, a portion above the lintel came loose and there was plaster everywhere. We couldn't just knock and enter. It had to look like a rescue in case Mr. Daku Man Singh hadn't yet been apprehended. Big scene. My last big scene in their crazy movie. Then the dinner where Nelson and I parted company, parted karma, carrying within each of us the vestiges of our intertwined fate, forever.

Epilogue

My father's name was George. I admired him without hesitation. He was an artist. Georgia is my middle name and I didn't use it for many years, but went by my first name, Julia, an unmistakably feminine name. But then I changed it, for I preferred the cachet of Georgia, often shortening it to "George." It felt racier than Julia.

We identify with notions, I believe. Indian or American, male or female, we exercise subtle imaginings of who we are and what it means. When I came to India, I was full of myself, feeling important with my project, brave, racy, and, in retrospect, quite hard. Karma seemed a little weak and unsure of himself in comparison but during the days before I left to come home again, it struck me that I was left in the company of seasoned objectivists when what I needed was a friend. Mandy, James, Hamid, Phoolan, Nelson, even Moona, once he had "crossed over," all had made conscious decisions to act and had stayed on their determined paths until the outcome had been reached. I realized at that last dinner together that I was different from them, that I never really knew what I was doing when I came to India. And then I didn't even know what it was I had done once it was over. But I *had* accomplished something that I could not have predetermined. I gained my independence. I stood up for myself in *my* final analysis, because I didn't carry on with Nelson.

This was not an easy decision to make. It took a friend to help me over the hump, and Karma was that friend. I felt closer to Karma than to any of them. Karma was not cold, and although he was as invested in the scheme as the rest of them, he has an evident practice of considering the whole, what he calls the sangha, or community of people.

I heard a lot about "the big picture" at the final dinner. Enough that I realized that when it comes to understanding life, I had been short-sighted; I was clearer when the events were close up, but irresponsibly vague when forced to imagine on a larger scale. I had to back up in order to focus — back *away* rather. Especially from Nelson.

Nelson might have put me on a backburner when he prioritized his duty to his brother above our "love," but he was nonetheless hurt when I told him that we were finished. He put up the argument that he had done all that he could to ensure that I would be safe. He said that he had had to endure the anxiety of knowing that something was going to happen to us, that he had known as we lay our heads down in the Thar Desert that evening that he, too, would be out cold, trusting to the organization that he and Urban Help had put into place. He pointed out the fact that it had *worked*, no one had suffered, really, except those who were targeted to fall, Dilly Willy and Mr. Daku Man Singh. No manner of my talking could help him to listen to what *I* believed he had done. It was his inability to concede to my perspective, even just to admit that what he had exposed me to wasn't fair, that made me decide to separate from him.

I have a different idea of how to "use" people now. When I first came to India, I thought that I could take an objective position toward the lives of others. I was going to research prostitution, an arrogant precept, expecting to turn the stories of other people into an accolade for myself. But instead, I have been used, and despite all of the sugaring on this bitter pill that I have swallowed — including the seduction of love — I resent having been a pawn. Inside each of us is the desire to be regal, to be effective, important in relation to our worlds.

Dahli, Ginni, Dharma — my "case studies" — by writing their stories, would I be taking away their self-determination? This was what Nelson took from me. He took from me my idea of what life should consist of — for me — and replaced it with what *he* believed my life should consist of. But this is what he was also fighting against, for his brother had been robbed of his life by those who felt that they could take away from him his self-determination and substitute it with their idea of how Norman could be used. My conscience feels clean. I am not going to turn Dahli, Ginni, and Dharma's lives into a story that exposes their shame. I am going to show how *they* became queens, how their bravery and self-sacrifice made them saints. How their karma made for a better dharma. At the outset, I was misguided. I am changed.

Karma, however, knew from the outset that what he did would affect anyone who was joined to him in a degree equal to that person's exposure to him — that karma was a matter of give and take on many levels. Karma's take on life is Indian, Nelson's American, and I came to feel more aligned to Karma, and less of a stranger to India.

Karma and I talked for hours after that final dinner meeting in Jagniwas Island. We talked all the way down to Mumbai on another rickety bus. We talked as I checked once again into the City Palace Hotel, and this time so did he, separate room, same status. I insisted upon it and he accepted the small gift of a good room.

I chose not to forgive Nelson — quite quickly. After all, he had set me up without my consent, and although my involvement in this larger picture helped to rectify an evil course of action, I now see clearly that it is more important to choose your lessons than to try to justify your retribution. Choice enables a moral and ethical decision that in turn creates karma. Nelson's way, as he involved me in it, was immoral and unethical.

The story of Mr. Daku Man Singh is serious in repercussions and pathetic in prejudice, and I am glad that he was apprehended, for Mr. Daku Man Singh believed that the way to exert control was to eliminate the "other" and reinforce those on the "inside." It was the premise of the ancient Thuggee cult — feed the goddess blood and she would reward with power. It was necessary to sacrifice someone in order to demonstrate power. Thuggee had the "magic" recipe with mandranioxide. THG had been developing an essential ingredient for an AIDS cocktail using Mandranioxide 8. If accepted and used in the United States, Daku Man Singh would be even richer than he already is — and more powerful. His inspiration was not to heal, however. It was to kill. He wanted to feed his bloodthirsty goddess with as much "weakness and immorality" as he could effectively control. Mandranioxide had been used as an anaesthetic, to dull pain, but it had not tested well. There were flaws — one of them being that the drug was hard to control. The dosage couldn't be set; it performed erratically. Some test subjects became euphoric. Some relaxed. And some — too many — died. I wonder how long it would have taken to discover that Mandranioxide 8 was a tainted drug, had "human sacrifice" not happened. But thankfully, Mr. Daku Man Singh was apprehended by the Indian police based on information from Urban Help, and his grand scheme never left the ground.

My final contribution in dispelling Mr. Daku Man Singh's distorted application of sacrifice is a self-conscious act. I told my story to Karma, as I perceived the events that happened to me between February 3 and March 3 of 2003. I felt that I had a healthy, transparent relationship with Karma, despite our cultural discrepancies, and I harboured no resentment toward his part in my having been "offered," against my instructions, in the sacrifice that helped to facilitate the final end to Daku Man Singh's evil scheme. Karma had believed that Nelson had told me everything from the outset.

I am not sure that Karma fully understood my story and I know that I will likely never really know what he went through, but telling Karma what I had perceived was very like being at confession. I felt lighter afterward, more like Julia, less like George.

It was from a feminine softness that I fell for Nelson and then was denied choice. Although he took advantage of my heat, my passion, he, too, was undoubtedly affected, and I still believe he is, in essence, a "good" man. I am thankful that my time in India and my time with him brought me a larger concept of my role in life.

My karma changed in India. It is only in retrospect that the imperceptible metamorphosis caused by "the slings and arrows of most outrageous fortune" can be understood. I believe that understanding is what Karma refers to as the dharma.

— *Julia Georgia Quercia*

Dharma, the law, has changed now. The ultimate truth is a higher reality. We are little beings and we cannot see this higher reality with clarity. We can only see it in our karma as it unfolds. The dharma upholds and supports our karma as we lead moral lives, each of us, for karma when in accordance with dharma, proceeds toward enlightenment.

I was pushed into *adharma*, where the acts were unnatural and immoral, when my not-father sold my sister to Dilly Willy and she died. I was called upon to correct the adharma and restore the order, and it was through Memsahib that I was given this opportunity. I could only see my karmic actions and the actions of those close to me. The steps we took served the creation of a new support, a new dharma.

In this way Memsahib and I loved each other and brought about a just retribution. But I am not sure that I understand her, nor that I have been able to capture her story. She seemed wobbly throughout, as if she never gained her footing on Indian ground. I thought that Nelson steadied her for a while, but she didn't stay with him and this showed me her strength.

She told me that she felt better by herself, and as she told me her story, I heard her bloom like the faint rustle of petals opening.

— *Karma Pradesh*

Acknowledgements

In the beginning it was Sheila Fruman, Gregory, Peter, and I in a groovy Land Rover driving overland from Turkey to India, where James, Ramone, Alexandro, and Timothy L. introduced me to a brothel in Bombay. Then a long skip on a pleasant Okanagan pond with Greta, Victor, and Christopher Oakes and all that was Headbones. A new path began in New York — Terry Williams, James Miller, Christopher Hitchens, Susan and Ramone, Amy, Peggy, Candida Royalle, Veronica Vera, and my intellectual interlocutor, Richard Fogarty, who traipsed around India with me for two months and still is by my side. Thoraya Mohammed introduced me to the women through their case histories, and without Action Aid and Sagir Malik's Ambassador their story would not have come to light. Peter Brigg edited with relish and spurs while Nancy Jain, Joan McClintock, and Toronto honed. Matt Stone wound the reel in to Napoleon Publishing with Sylvia, Allister, and Emma. Allison and Michael at Dundurn placed the bow on the package. Thank you for the gift of a fertile destiny.

Of Related Interest

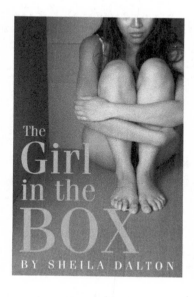

The Girl in the Box
by Sheila Dalton
978-1926607269 $22.99

A mute Mayan girl held captive in a crate in the Guatemalan jungle, a big-city psychoanalyst with a rescue complex, and a journalist with a broken heart are the characters in Sheila Dalton's second literary novel. Inez, a traumatized young Mayan woman originally from Guatemala, has killed Caitlin's partner, leaving Caitlin to figure out why.

Six Metres of Pavement
by Farzana Doctor
978-1554887675 $22.99

Ismail Boxwala made the worst mistake of his life one summer morning 20 years ago: he forgot his baby daughter in the back seat of his car. After her tragic death, he struggles to continue living through a divorce, years of heavy drinking, and sex with strangers. But his story begins to change after he reluctantly befriends two women.

Available at your favourite bookseller.

DUNDURN

www.dundurn.com

What did you think of this book?
Visit *www.dundurn.com* for reviews, videos, updates, and more!

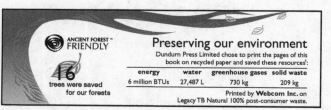

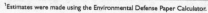